# From the Dragon Lord's Library

*Nicole Petit*
*Curator*

FROM THE DRAGON LORD'S LIBRARY
AN 18THWALL PRODUCTIONS BOOK PUBLISHED BY
ARRANGEMENT WITH NICOLE PETIT
VERBA MEA IN MANIBUS
DESIDERIUM MEUM
ISBN-13: 978-0692618981
ISBN-10: 0692618988
COVER BY MORGAN FITZSIMONS          ..
TEXT COPYRIGHT
INTRODUCTION © NICOLE PETIT
THE DRAGON, FLY © JILLY PADDOCK
AFTER THE DRAGON © JOANNA HOYT
CALL OF GOLD © CLAIRE DAVON
DRAGONFLY SHADOWS © J. PATRICK ALLEN
DREAMING OF DRAGON WINGS © T. FOX DUNHAM
TIPPING THE SCALES © DORIAN GRAVES
HOW THE DRAGON WON A BATTLE IN THE NEVER-ENDING WAR © DENAROSE FUUSHIMA
THE DRAGON'S CLAUSE © KELLY A. HARMON
LIZARD CLAW © E. A.FOW
BLOSSOM WAR © ROBERT W. CALDWELL
THE DYING DRAGON © JIM LEE

## PUBLISHER'S NOTE

# Table of Contents

# The Dragon, Fly
*Jilly Paddock*

She sits on a pinnacle of honeycombed stone, a finger
stabbing insolent into the heavens, so frost-eaten and wind-
worn it seems that the fragile rock must splinter beneath her
weight. Maybe it would fall were she not stick-thin, her
flesh eroded away much as the rock has been, her skin
tanned to the sallow colour of the land. She might have
been a carving of the ancient, desert peoples, an earth-spirit
or air-walker out of their fire-told tales, shaped by a
forgotten hand in the friable, ochre sandstone, but for her
wispy halo of hair, bleached white now under the fierce
suns, and the bright flicker of her eyes. They say she has sat
thus for twenty years, with no shelter under the wild sky, a
stylite, unmoving; a saint on her pillar of stone.

Far to the west, at the suns-set edge of the world, is a
dark smudge of a city, ten days journey away across the
sharp sands on camel-back, only two by skim-raft.
Sometimes they venture out here, the tourists, to stare and
wonder at her in this barren place, leaving only footprints
and litter, or little, senseless scrawlings in the buttery rock.
Then again, the dragons are here too, and perhaps it is only

that presence which tempts humanity so far from the safety of its city, to squint up into the brilliance of the twin suns, to gawp and cry out at alien, delicate wings dipping through a cobalt sky.

The Dragons of Teusza!

The explorers who first charted this world, those who weighed and measured its grains of sand, and who sifted and catalogued its beasts, birds and flowers–such narrow-souled creatures!–were blind to the glory of Teusza's winged-folk. Perhaps the dragons hid from them; whatever the way of it, the colonists were on-world for many handfuls of seasons before discovering that they were not the sole owners of Teusza's skies.

Tell then of dragons: sing of their forms and colours!

Yes, sing of the wondrous, liquid contours of them, of the sudden, fierce lightness of them, of the double sunlight dribbling in rainbows along their scales! Two metres long, from lashing tail-tip to the curve of their whiskers. Yes, whiskers, bristling furiously from their narrow snouts, like any Earthly cat. Strap-thin bodies, fluid and seemingly boneless, serpentine and sinuous; large, yet not large enough for any human to dream of riding them, for not even an infant could cling to such smooth, rippling backs.

Wings like fragile, rustling paper, appearing too insubstantial to bear any weight, and little, delicate limbs, eight in all, each blessed with a long, six-fingered hand.

Ah, but the colours of them, the copper blues, the lethal lead greens and iron oxide reds! Describe them on paper: black-inked words will never convey their fearful swiftness or their terrible grace, nor tell how the sight of them tears at the human heart, twisting it in pincers of joy.

What supports them in the thin airs of the desert plateau? Certainly not those absurd wings, since they scarcely need to beat them to remain suspended in the ether, floating without effort, sometimes hanging motionless and curled asleep in mid-air. Perhaps they are hollow-boned, perhaps lifted by internal sacs of some light gas. Some have said that they fly by means of mind or magic, and no life-scientist has any evidence to contradict such lunatic supposition, since no dragon has ever suffered capture. No net or trap can hold them, no drugged dart or bullet touch them in flight, not even dead do they yield up their secrets, for no dragon-corpse has ever been found on the bare plains.

Tell now of the ways of dragons!

Tell of how they spiral up through the air, until it thins,

rarefies and fades altogether, until they wheel, like a cloud of iridescent soap-bubbles, under the cold, sharp stars, It seems to amuse them to mob the spacecraft that ply to and fro from Teusza, playing chicken with the pilot's nerves, and sometimes riding the fiery bow-waves of re-entry, as dolphins do, careless of the incandescence, the vacuum, the gravity, as if such physical things have no meaning for them. Perhaps they do not breathe. How else could they thrive in such harshness? A mystery then, Teusza's mythical creatures, and drawing all the more attention because of that.

And is there no more to tell of dragons?

They have no love for humankind, an opinion they express with needle-tooth and razor-claw if required to, although their preference is to avoid man rather than harm him. Some subtle cunning warns them that to kill their un-friends will invite more determined hunting, so they leave their victims skin-scarred, perhaps missing an eye, invariably alive. The tourists they tolerate, preening and displaying in front of their audience with indifferent vanity, provided that the visitors don't stay too long. Of all humanity, only the solitary woman, the hermit, will they allow to remain in their lands.

8

What of her, that lonely woman? How does she live in the heart of the desert, trapped on the tip of her pillar?

The dragons feed her, plucking fruit for her from orchards that lie beyond the mountains, bringing her fat, greasy insects that they snap on the wing or choice slivers of raw meat from their prey. Sometimes little troops of them raid the nomad camps to steal fresh-baked cakes or scraps of fish left to dry in the suns. All of this she accepts gravely, eating even the foul without protest or prejudice. Water they carry to her, cupping it in folds of their wings and letting her lap from the saucers of their flesh. The indigenous peoples have built a little shrine at the foot of her pinnacle, where they leave food for her when they pass by, their reward a glimpse of the dragons' sky-dance.

They say that once a young man came to her pillar and dared to scale it, that the dragons didn't pluck him from the rock face and hurl him down. And is it so?

He was tall and strong, proud of that strength, proud of the stretch of his arm and the pull of his muscles. His name was Tyagi and his skin was black, but his long hair was yellower than the desert. The pillar he climbed for a dare; it took him three hours and much sweat, and he tested himself on the raw edge of fear each time his hand slipped from a hold or the dry rock fell to powder under his fingers. By the time he flopped over the rim of the summit he was near exhaustion, his hands flayed and bleeding, his sides heaving with exertion. All the while, the dragons looked on.

She had been there a little less than a year then. Her skin was roughened yet not dried up by the winds and her hair was still brown, the dry brown of dead autumn grass.

"Good day, lady," panted Tyagi, for he was polite and besides, having climbed so far to view the hermit, he found that he liked what he saw.

Eyes like fallen pieces of sky gazed past him and there was no expression on her face. It was as still and serene as the land is, touched by humanity but enduring.

"You have a fine view!" Tyagi observed, unabashed by her silence, settling himself for a rest before his descent. "On a fine day such as today it's grand to be up here but in the rain and wind, that must be a different matter, and, pardon me for bringing the subject up, what will you do when winter sweeps the plateau with snow?"

The dragons began to sing then, their uncanny purring hymn to the empty skies, and they spiralled up to dance a measure on the wind. The young man had no choice but to watch, as if they had laid a spell on him. She watched also, and did a fragment of a smile touch her lips?

"When the snow falls, they will keep it from my head."

Tyagi started at the sound of her voice, the sound of dead leaves scratching on a pane of glass, the sound of winter's ice strangling the ripples on a lake. She spoke slowly, as if she'd unremembered human speech. The dragons floated close, gazing at her out of one eye and then the other, as if amazed at the sudden rasp of her voice.

"They care for me." This time she did smile, briefly, as if it made her cheeks hurt. "This they have done ever since I came here."

Tyagi said softly, "And where did you come from?"

She wrenched her sky-hued eyes from the cluster of dragons and looked at him for the first time. "Everywhere and everywhere. I have forgotten the names."

Tyagi folded his long legs under him, finding comfort on the bare bones of rock in the hope of a long tale. "But you have a name?"

"My father called me Teusza. He loved this world and dreamed of coming here." She sighed and one of the dragons unravelled from the flock and swam over to her, crooning and draping itself across her thin shoulders like a ragged leather cape. Tyagi tried not to stare at it, for the dragons never touched the ground and the legends said that to do so was bane to them. The awful nearness of the beast burned his eyes, much as staring at a light-source will, the play of suns-light on its red-copper, blood-ruby and rosy-quartz scales dazzling and hypnotic. The woman reached up and scratched its chin absently, then continued to speak. "I was born on the far side of the sky, in a black pit of a city, a cold, fearsome place where we starved and struggled through what passed for life, my father and I, alone. I knew no mother–she left us."

Tyagi let her rest for a little after so long a speech. "Tell me of your father."

"My father was a great man. He was a weaver of tales, a maker of songs. There was a time when we lived at the court of a merchant-prince, a time of riches, comfort and joy, but the world changed for the worst and our fortunes changed with it. My father's skills were belittled, scorned, and he turned his hand to the common trades to feed us, spending his days in mines or factories. For years we survived, sustained by his dreams. Through all the bleak, hungry nights he would sit in the darkness and tell me of Teusza and the dragons." She shivered and the wonder draped about her gaunt body hummed gently to her. "I can still hear his voice, the music of it and how his words would sparkle in the misery of the city. He did so want to come here and I believe he would have, except that he died."

The dragon moaned, somehow in tune with the sorrow in her eyes. Tyagi did not dare to speak, she looked so distant and vulnerable.

"These were his last words to me," Teusza continued. " 'Go away from this terrible place,' he said. 'Don't let them kill you with their indifference, as they've destroyed me. Leave, and if you can, go to the world that I named you for.' I promised to obey–out of love I took up the burden of his geas. I had to sell his body, all of the marketable pieces, until I had enough money to leave. His skull I had them burn and carried that small part of him away with me. Many more empty years passed before I came here. I buried my father's ashes at the base of this rock, where he may rest and dream for eternity, and then I climbed up to get a better view of the dragons."

Tyagi waited for some minutes, but she was silent, having reached the end of her history. "And you stayed here?"

"I was carried here by a promise born out of my father's longing. It wasn't my dream, but I was curious to see what had sustained his hopes for so long. Only when I climbed up here and looked out over the desert did I realise the truth of it, and know that I'd come home."

The dragon blew into her ear, tickling her with its frivolous whiskers, and she laughed, sweet and high as a child would, at which the serpent-thing sprang from her, darting up from its perch and somersaulting suns-ward.

"Scant comfort for a home." The young man brushed the gritty sand from his skin, where it had adhered and indented his flesh. "Don't you miss warmth, shelter, companionship?"

"I've friends in abundance." She waved at the dragons, who had moved a small distance away to investigate the arrival of a skim-raft. "I have a name for each of them: the bluest one is Be, the green-and-gold, Do, that brown pair there are Dance and Leap. My favourite of them all, my special friend, the largest red who was here just now is called Fly."

Down in the desert the raft had stopped and its occupants were waging war on the dragons. Tyagi looked on in horror at the blue-green stabs of lasers and the little

14

sparkling clouds of propellant gas from hand-held missile-firers. For all the ferocity of the attack none of the dragons appeared to have been touched.

"They cannot hurt them," Teusza said, smiling, as if the hunters were playing a harmless game. "Sometimes I don't believe that men will ever accept that fact."

"Are the beasts then indestructible?"

"The dragons are," the girl said, as if that explained all of their mystery. "They are our dreams."

The skirmish went on for the best part of half an hour, until the dragons tired of dancing targets for the weapons spitting death, dived in close to deliver a few scratches to indicate their displeasure and climbed into the vault of the sky in a lazy helix, like birds slouching on a thermal. The hunters limped their raft back towards the city.

"This is no kind of life for a young woman like you." Tyagi declared. "What if a stray dart or beam should injure you?"

"My friends would not permit it."

Tyagi shook his head. "Come down with me, Teusza. I'll take you back to the city and take care of you. You should have a man of your own and children by now. You deserve more than a stump of sandblasted rock."

"I have all that I need," she returned, with infuriating content. "For empty years of my life all that kept me alive was the memory of my father's dream. Now I'm living it."

The suns had raced to the horizon and were vying with each other to splash spoonfuls of red and orange across the sky, while one guilty, premature star glared disdainfully down from its zenith, a prim, barren aunt embarrassed by the behaviour of children.

"I must go, before it grows too dark to climb down." Tyagi shivered at the bright edge of the twilight wind. "Please come with me."

The girl merely shook her head. Tyagi shrugged and eased himself past the overhang, but he'd scarcely inched a span down the cliff when a pair of strong, wiry hands caught him under his arms and a second set gripped his belt, lifting him away from the powdery rock. The young man cried out and looked up into the fanged and feline-smiling ruby face of the dragon Fly. The shock of being suspended in clear air and the warm strangeness of the creature's touch kept him frozen throughout the lazy spiral to the plain, although his pulse beat in his throat, as a fox might thrash in a snare. As soon as his toes touched solid ground, the dragon released him and he could breathe again. He all but ran away from the rock outcrop, not daring to look back until he had covered several hundred metres.

She sat there with the crimson beast draped about her shoulders and when she saw him turn, she raised her hand in a cheery wave.

And did he love her then, black Tyagi, lion-man?

Yes, although he didn't know it. He'd loved her from that first look into the sky-pools of her eyes. Years later he found a girl to wed, with oak-leaf hair and eyes like his rock-bound hermit, yet he knew how he deceived himself and he was never truly happy.

And what became of her, beast-beloved, imprisoned by her own will on that insolent finger of stone?

She sat with the broken land about her, as if atop the mast of a wrecked ship, surveying its shattered spars and timbers, but mostly she watched her dragons. They say she sat there, unmoving, for a century or maybe more, until a man came and climbed the pillar for a second time. Tyagi's grandson, they say he was, and as proud and strong as his sire. Over many hours he sweated and strained his way up and when he reached the summit he found only the desiccated husk of a woman's body that fell to dust when he touched it, while the dragons looked on and sang their inhuman dirge.

"And is that the end of the tale?" asked the unborn Child. "Didn't you promise me a happy ending?"

"As the peasants tell it the saint of the pillar didn't die and to this day she, or perhaps the ghost of her, may still be seen, sitting cross-legged on the buttery rock. Yet others say that she became one of the creatures she so loved, a gold-scaled dragon, and that she remains there still, flying in the dry desert air."

"And is that true?"

"Who can say?" said the Mother, with a twitch of her whiskers and a lash of her butter-gold tail. "No man has ever counted the dragons of Teusza."

# After the Dragon

*Joanna Hoyt*

No one in the Seven Villages had ever seen the Dragon, but
we all knew that our lives were held in its life like embers
in a wildfire or tears in the sea. We all recited the Gifts of
the Dragon at the spring festival: rain, fire, fear, love, birth,
death, dreams, fertile ground.

It was death that most of the goatherds thought of one
morning late in the dry season when the colors brightened
around them, when each grass-blade stood above its own
sharp shadow. They ran down the slope toward the spring
and the stone house. Neither offered sure protection. No
water could bear the brightness of the Dragon's reflection;
if the Dragon passed straight overhead water would rise in
golden steam, beautiful, but deadly hot, and where Dragon-
fire first fell it burned stone like wood. Still, water and
stone would keep people safe if they were only at the edges
of a spreading grass-fire. So they ran.

But Nesé of Corlé, forty years old and bold as a child,
ran up the esker, her cloak flapping winglike in the Dragon-
wind, her eyes raised to a sky blue-bright as the base of a

flame. When the light and wind were too much to bear she shut her eyes and lay down on the hilltop, felt the wind and heat pressing her into the earth, lay still until the first great raindrops fell, hot from the Dragon's passing.

She opened her eyes to a world soaked and shining. Smoke shot with sparks rose far away to her left where the Dragon-fire had struck on the open ridgetop. The grass grew visibly around her, stretching up into the golden rain. A man stood on her right, soaked and shining. He was a neighbor, she had seen him every day for forty years, but when she looked at him in the Dragon-light she thought she had never really seen him before.

That afternoon the villagers came to see the burned ground. Grass, trees and stones had turned to the black ash that would be next year's cropland. No other soil bore as richly as Dragon-tilth. Seven days later the black soil was covered with the silver stems and red-gold blossoms of semelokë, the fire-flower. Three weeks later the semelokë dissolved into white dust and the sowers came to plant grain.

Eight months later Nesé's twins were born: first Émon, then Anelé who became my mother. Their father was not named, according to the custom; they were said to have been gotten by the Dragon. The twins were gifted like all Dragon-children, and Nesé's husband learned to be almost as glad and proud of them as of his own sons and daughters.

Émon was deft-handed, dark-haired and silver-eyed. He said little, but he remembered everything. Anelé's hair was red-gold like semelokë flowers, and she feared nothing. Without Émon Anelé might have broken arms and legs as she climbed trees and scrambled up screes and boulders. Without Anelé Émon might never have learned to climb.

They were always together as children. Later, when Émon's skill took him to the smithy and Anelé's took her into the fields, they still spoke from mind to mind, calling in delight at his first successful mending, at her first finding of the zufara seeds that cured fever, calling in pain when Émon burned his hand, when Anelé twisted her ankle. Such bonding was not uncommon between young children, especially the Dragon-got, but as Émon and Anelé grew older the bond between them strengthened.

Anelé was herb-gathering alone late in the dry season in her eighteenth year when the air quivered around her and the hairs rose on her neck and arms. She knew what it was and she ran to meet it. Émon, three leagues away shoeing a horse under the old smith's eye, felt her delight and stumbled blindly out the door, calling in his mind to Anelé, *Come back! It isn't safe!*

She heard him, even then, and laughed a little: *Émon, it's all right!* Then the brightness filled her mind, leaving no room for him.

He was still sitting in the dust outside the smithy when Anelé and Doren of Ochlé walked into the village hand in hand, wet and laughing and with eyes only for each other. Émon rose and wished their happiness politely, but he held his mind closed against Anelé. It was a grief to her, even then.

He forgave her as much as he could. He danced at her wedding and gave her a pendant shaped like a zufara blossom. Sometimes their minds still touched. When Émon dropped a red-hot ox shoe on his foot Anelé heard his cry of pain, took the mare over the ridge to Corlé and dressed his foot. When Anelé would have gone back to work in the fields when she was still weak after bearing me, Uncle Émon felt her weariness and persuaded her to rest longer. But Émon thought of Anelé more often than she thought of him; often her mind was full of Doren, or of me and my brothers and sisters, or of the memory of the Dragon-light. I think she never knew how much this hurt him.

I was nine years old, and nine leagues away in Lailé with my father's sister Maillé, when Uncle Émon woke out of deep sleep. He thought that he rose from his bed, went to the door and looked out at the stars, which were thick as a swarm of midges and bright as...As the memory of that other light stirred in his mind he realized that the doorway through which he looked was narrower than that of the house behind the smithy, and it looked, not over a yard beaten flat by the feet of waiting horses, but across a kitchen garden to a stream. Then Émon understood that he was asleep, that it was Anelé who looked out into the shining night, Anelé who laughed, poised to run out into the gathering brightness.

*No, Anelé!* my uncle called. *Doren! The children! There's danger for them! Get them to the stream!*

Anelé heard. She took my infant sister Ossé in her arms, shook my father's shoulder, shouted to the other children, and took a few steps downhill before the fire fell.

Next morning a farmer with a broken harness ring went through the golden rain to Émon's smithy and found it deserted. He thought my uncle had overslept. He called under Émon's window. Finally he forced the door open.

23

Émon lay abed, moaning like a wounded beast. The farmer ran for Émon's half-sister, my Aunt Lissé. She laid her hands on his skin, felt his fever, gave him a cooling draught and sent the farmer to Ochlé for Anelé. The farmer came back alone as the light failed and told her that Ochlé was gone.

"Gone," my uncle repeated. That was all he said while the semelokë grew and bloomed. He ate food and took medicine when it was put in front of him. The fever passed, but his will didn't come back. Lissé told him to get up and get dressed and come to the death-mind. He didn't answer. She dressed him and led him by the hand to the memorial ground and the dancing-lawn. When she put semelokë blossoms in his hands he threw them down. That was the only spark of life he showed until he saw me.

I was there with Aunt Maillé, flowers in my arms and confusion in my mind. I had something of my mother's dreaming gift; I had felt her pain at the end, and her grief for her children's pain, and also her wild improbable joy…and no thought of me at all. There at the death-mind I felt my pain echoing from somewhere outside me. I looked up to see my uncle running toward me. "Anelé!"

"No, Émon," Lissé said. "It's Lirié. Her daughter. The

oldest. Anelé is gone."

I wanted to hold my uncle, who had been closer to my mother than anyone else I knew. I wanted to know why he had called me by her name. He turned away from me.

Everyone always came to the festival of quickening, to the death-mind and the dancing and the song of the Dragon's gifts. Even the old and the sick came to help make the renewing. But my uncle Émon pushed through the crowd and started walking home. Aunt Lissé called after him. He ignored her. His half-brothers caught his shoulders. He pulled away. They had to let him go.

He went back to work after that, but he did not speak beyond what the work required. I stayed with Aunt Lissé. When I passed the smithy I felt Émon's eyes on me, but all through the months of rain and the month of harvest and the gathering drought he did not speak to me.

That didn't keep his secrets from me. After that meeting at the festival my mind knew the feel of him, and sometimes I shared his memories and dreams as I had shared my mother's. More than I had shared my mother's. She loved me, but her fears and her wants were often beyond my understanding. But Uncle Émon wanted her back as much as I did; perhaps even more than I did, which shamed me somehow. From my own memory of my mother brewing a cooling draught when I was fevered I slipped into my uncle's memory of the day when he burned himself and she came back for him, of the day he lost her to Doren, and then we came back together to the day we lost her to the Dragon. I couldn't tell whether he knew that I moved in his mind with him or whether he took me for my mother's ghost.

The dry season wore on and we waited for the Dragon-rain. One day when Aunt Lissé came to bring Émon his lunch he reached out for her.

"Émon, are you all right?"

"It's hard. Hard…waiting."

"Waiting to heal, sure. You're not the only one who's grieved over Anelé. Oh, I know, it's hardest for you, you were closest. More like what I felt, maybe, when I lost my Susté to the fever, just three days old. I wanted to die too, to go with her. And then the Dragon passed again, and the rains came, and there was the dancing, and I knew I might as well go on."

"No," my uncle said. "Not to heal. Waiting…for it to come again…to lose…" He stared into her eyes, willing her

26

to understand. It was a way he and my mother both had, expecting others to understand them wordlessly as they understood each other. It had always maddened Aunt Lissé. She pulled away from him.

He began to talk to other people. To Merié, who had been betrothed to Marn until he met Sulé under the dragon-light; to Corm, whose only son had died in the fire that took Ochlé; to Halben, who was jealous of Sofgren his older brother, a Dragon-got child with a gift of storytelling that left the listeners blind and deaf to all else until the story ended.

"What do we wait for so eagerly?" Émon said to them. "Why should we celebrate" I was clear on the other side of the village then, milking one of Aunt Lissé's goats, but I heard him in my mind.

"How can we not?" Halben answered. "The Dragon's always been. Always will be."

"More's the pity," my uncle answered, turning back to the forge.

It might have stayed at that if it hadn't been for the man who came down the river from somewhere clear outside the

Seven Villages. He didn't look dangerous—a red-haired weak-chinned man in a pack-boat laden with trade goods. His cloth was soft and pretty but it wouldn't wear like our mohair; his pottery was fine enough, but it didn't have the comfortable shapes of the jars we patted out of clay from the riverbank. But he also brought spices that we'd never tasted before, that burst in the mouth like lightning or opened slow and rich as buds, and metals Uncle Émon hadn't seen. The trader stopped a week with Uncle Émon, talking about his craft—and other things.

The trader came from a place where there was no Dragon. Without Dragon-tilth they had to build soil slowly and carefully, with manure and the ash of man-made fires. With no Dragon to celebrate, they made do with festivals in honor of good harvests or rich trading voyages. They seemed content with that shadow-life. *Poor things*, Aunt Lissé said. Most agreed with her. But a light came back into Uncle Émon's eyes. He spoke to others as he'd spoken to Merié and Corm and Halben, and he worked late at nights on some project of his own which no one ever saw.

I heard the adults talking about him when they thought I was asleep. One night their talk ran in and out of my dreams, and when I woke and found them still at it I got up and said "I know what Uncle Émon's doing. He wants to stop the Dragon."

"Hush, don't speak an ill word. You were dreaming."

"I know!"

"There's no one can stop the Dragon. He might as well try and stop the sun. He knows that; he's no fool, your Uncle Émon. He just...loved your mother very much."

"So did Lirié love her mother very much, but she's wise enough to let her go." That was Lissé. "Don't you go telling her that love means madness."

"Émon isn't mad!"

I went back to bed and let them argue. But I knew what I knew.

Uncle Émon didn't go to the next quickening festival, though his sisters nagged him. In earlier years Émon had helped in the fields, not having enough smith-work to keep him, though he'd avoided the rich soil that had once been Ochlé. But that year he cleared a patch that hadn't been burned in living memory and worked it alone. It was hard work—he dug the tough sod up himself as the stranger said men did in his country, instead of using the soft ashland— and poor soil, bearing scanty fruit and grain; nevertheless that was where he worked, and that was what he ate.

That, and the game he hunted. He'd never been one for hunting, but he drove himself late and early and managed, from time to time, to bring home deer at first, squirrels and rabbits as his aim improved. His neighbors reminded him that they'd always feed him gladly, and that it was a nuisance not knowing when he'd be at the forge. He shrugged.

He did that for a year, and then as the waiting for the dragon-rains began again he disappeared for a day. *Hunting again*, Aunt Lissé said. Two days. *Hunting unsuccessfully, and too proud to come home empty-handed, the fool*, she said. Three days. "Dragon-hunting," I said.

"What nonsense are you talking now?"

"The trader said they didn't have a Dragon in the place where he came from, but they had stories about dragons. Bad dragons."

"No ill words from you, miss. The Dragon's more than good or bad, and you know it."

"But the trader didn't know. He said they were bad. He said people killed them. Good people. Brave people. Uncle Émon was listening with his eyes lit up."

Aunt Lissé scolded me for listening to what wasn't my business, but she took off for the high ridge right after breakfast. Checking on her son Rethen and the goatherds, she said. Looking for Uncle Émon, I knew. I went after her. Well, not after her, after him. I thought back to my mother, to her hurt and her joy and her having no place for me. I waited until I felt the memory echoing from somewhere outside my head, and I went toward that feeling.

As I got closer the memory outside me got hotter and hurt more, like the place where I drove the thorn in and wouldn't tell Aunt Lissé until I started to have the fever and shakes. The memory hurt even worse than that. I didn't notice the changing air until the bright rain fell.

I found Uncle Émon before the rain cooled on my skin. He slumped in the grass clutching a throwing-spear bigger than any I'd seen before—and different-colored. He must have made it with metal he got from the trader, from the place where they thought they could kill dragons. He hadn't killed anything. He was shaking.

"It's gone now, Uncle Émon," I said. "Come home."

He didn't open his eyes. "I couldn't even stand to face it. I had to, and I couldn't."

"Nobody can. Even she couldn't."

We both knew who *she* was.

"And she was there," he said, his voice shaking too.

"She was there. With that thing. In it! She…she called to me…it wasn't really her…but it was…" He opened his eyes and stared at me the way he had two years before.

"Anelé?"

"No!" I said. I turned from him and ran away down the steep slope, stumbling and lurching. I ran straight into Aunt Lissé.

"He's up there. He's crazy. I want to go home."

She carried me home, and for once she didn't scold me. My uncle dragged himself back late that night. He looked like a sick dog for a while. Then he seemed to come back to himself. I didn't want to know why; I shut my mind against him, knowing I'd lied to Aunt Lissé. He wasn't crazy. What he'd said about my mother being there inside the Dragon—that was true.

He worked his meager ground again that summer, and he kept disappearing into the woods, but he didn't come back with game. I knew where he went. I couldn't help seeing in dreams how he went through the berry-bramble and the valley with the broken pines, down to the Black Lake.

The Black Lake! The grown-ups didn't talk about it much in front of us children, but they did tell us we were never to go there and we weren't to talk about it. We made up the rest. The way our stories went, the Black Lake was bitter cold in the height of summer, and dark under the brightest sky, and you could kneel by it at any angle to the light and never see your reflection in its ice-smooth surface. That was more frightening, maybe, then the ghasts and afreets and other foul creatures we imagined. When I heard the stories I shrieked most at the parts about the monsters, but when I dreamed of the lake there was only the dark and the cold and the long blind waiting.

When I first dreamed of Uncle Émon at the Black Lake there weren't any monsters, but he was afraid. He came out of the pines, saw the black water, and shivered as if he'd swallowed ice. He tried to make his feet take him closer but they wouldn't go. Finally he turned back into the tree-shadows, hanging his head, dog-sick again. I felt the shame twisting his throat, the same shame he'd felt when he couldn't stand to face the dragon-light. I was sorry for him, but I was glad too. I'd wanted him not to go any closer to that water almost as badly as he'd wanted it himself.

Twice more he went and shook and turned away. The last time he knew he couldn't make himself go any closer. But seven days later he went through the broken pines again. Not to the clear land around the lake. He went uphill, northward, until he came to a clear little stream that ran down into the lake. The stream itself looked safe enough. He didn't fear it, and when he drank its water from his cupped hands it was sweet. He looked again at the hill above him and below him. I didn't know what he was thinking, but I felt what he felt; a grim little satisfaction, and a great grim patience that had grown to fill part of the aching hole that my mother's death had made.

He stayed in the village for the next three weeks except for short hunting trips, and he sang again at his forge. Not the village songs that all came back to the Dragon sooner or later, but a little song with no words and barely any tune that slowed and quickened in time with his work. He was taken up with his work and didn't notice me. He also didn't notice that the hot-metal smell of the forge was just a little bit like Dragon-scent.

One day, though, he dunked an ox-shoe hot and hissing into the cooling pail and turned his head toward the door to keep the steam out of his eyes, and he saw me. Something moved behind his eyes and inside my chest. I was afraid he'd call me by my mother's name again. He didn't speak, and suddenly he was farther away than if he'd closed the door between us. I realized then that I had thought I'd shut him from my mind, but it might have been the other way around.

I went to Aunt Lissé that night and told her that Uncle Émon had gone near the Black Lake and it had put a spell on him, and that he was still trying to do something crazy about the Dragon. She grabbed my shoulder, dug her fingers right into my bones and asked what kind of a fool I was to go near the Black Lake. I said I hadn't gone, I'd only seen it because Uncle Émon was there. She said if anything was crazy it was me, a half-grown girl, believing every unholy thing I dreamed. We both said, and then shouted, things we didn't really mean. She stormed out of the house. I tried to settle myself and reach in my mind for my uncle.

I found my aunt as well. They were together in his scraggy little vegetable patch. He weeded and kept his eyes on his hands. She glared at him.

"What cursed nonsense you're up to I'm sure I don't know, but what poor Anelé would think if she could see you now…"

He straightened and looked at her. His eyes were as black as the lake. She wasn't reflected in them. I felt him pulling that black cold over himself to keep himself from hitting her. He spoke very quietly.

"You never were one for minding your own business, were you? And now you'll tell the village. Don't trouble. I'll tell them. Have them come to me tonight. I'll tell them all."

He did. He stood there in the torchlight and he told us how he'd found a safe place for us, a place where the Dragon couldn't come and hurt us ever again.

They told him he was mad; not only Aunt Lissé, but all the village elders. They said the Dragon was life to us as well as death, and it was unchancy and ungrateful to speak against it. They said, too, that it was foolish to think we could hide from it, there was no other power to match it.

"Except the Black Lake," I said. "Where Uncle Émon's been."

"Except the Black Lake," he said. "I doubt that would melt away even at the Dragon's coming."

They said they couldn't live there, it was cursed, and anyway they couldn't drink the water. He said they didn't have to drink it. He told them about the stream, and how he could cut a channel down into the valley land, and how if we burned the pinewood we'd have ashland of our own. He told them, too, about caves—I hadn't seen him finding those; he must have shut me out—that could protect us from fire.

"You've seen the places where the Dragon-fire melted the stone."

"These caves are deeper. And the lake flows into the deepest ones."

"That place is cursed."

"All our lives we've lived under a curse, and called it a blessing. Haven't we? Merié? Halben? Corm?"

Halben and Merié nodded. Corm trembled and shook his head.

"Yes. No. Émon, how can I answer that either way, when my son's gone back into it? But the Black Lake…there's nothing I love in there."

The talking was long and angry, and I lost the thread of the words as their loves and fears and angers twisted round me in the dark. But in the end no one else would go with him. Merié and Corm wept, and Halben shook like a man palsied and wouldn't say yea or nay, and the others blamed my uncle for clinging to his grief instead of letting it go back into the Dragon-soil. Merié's husband, who knew well that his wife loved him less than she loved the man she lost to a dragon-love, said Émon had brought back a curse from the lake and he was sickening the village with it, and he should be sent out.

My uncle called the lake-cold to his mind again. He was still and silent for a long time, but everyone felt the cold strength seeping out from him. Finally he said "You can't send me. I will go."

I was often angry with Aunt Lissé, but I loved her then: she was afraid, but she found her voice and begged him to stay. I knew she couldn't keep him, but I knew the love and the courage that made her try. I knew I should have said what she said, but I didn't love him enough. I almost hated him because my mother in her last few moments had thought of him, had spoken in her mind to him and not to me. I thought that Uncle Émon knew my unlove, that that was why he looked coldly at me and walked away. Now I think maybe the unlove, like the closed door in the mind, started from his side, as he resented the child conceived the first time his sister turned her mind away from him.

He went away alone. Aunt Lissé went to see him every sennight, carrying her semelokë pendant and murmuring the Dragon-words to keep off curses, and also carrying grain and vegetables. Émon had begun to fell trees in the valley to make the ashland he had spoken of, though it was far from planting time. Far too much ashland, Aunt Lissé told me, for one man to tend.

"He still thinks we'll go and live there with him."

"Poor man! He's lost his wits sure, though why it should happen now, after all these years…"

"Maybe he's right."

She chided me then and said she should know better than to talk about such things to a mooncalf child. But after each visit to Émon she talked to me again. He was ashamed to take food from her, that was plain, and yet he kept on doing it. He had to; plants good for gathering did not grow near the Black Lake, and wild beasts never went to drink there. She thought eventually she'd shame him into coming home. I knew that he thought he would have something to give back to her, to all of us, that would more than make up for what he took. I didn't want to know what that was. I pushed it away as the harvest was gathered, as the dry season wore on.

I woke up in the middle of the night knowing what he was going to do. I lay awake and stared out the window at the small hard stars, trying to send a message back into his mind, but I ran into a wall of fear like the one he ran into when he first saw the Black Lake. When the sickness of it passed off enough to let me stand I went to Aunt Lissé and

39

shook her awake.

"We have to go to Uncle Émon now. We have to stop him."

"What?"

"We have to stop him. He's going to try to kill the Dragon again."

"He can't, child. He already found that out. And it didn't kill him the last time he tried, so likely it won't now either, even if he's witless enough to try again; and that's all out of our hands, so we might as well get our sleep and keep on doing what's ours to do."

"No! It's different now. He's at the lake, he's different, it's different."

"You're not making sense, Lirié. I know you're upset, but you're not making sense. Lie down, and we'll reason it out in the morning."

"There isn't time!"

She went to the door and looked out. "It's no brighter than usual."

"I can't see it either, but Uncle Émon can feel it coming, and I can too."

"Then you should be going to the springhouse, not fretting about your mad uncle!" She meant well, I knew that, but I didn't have very much of my mind free to think about it with, being full of my uncle and my mother and the Dragon and a hot hurting blend of fear and blame and wanting and delight that might have been theirs or my own. I pulled on my sandals and my cloak and ran out the door.

She shouted after me, and then she ran after me, but I had grown faster as she grew slower. By the time she'd gotten the sleep out of her eyes and the shoes onto her feet I had a head start. Her voice faded behind me as I crashed through the brush toward where my uncle waited on the high fell above the Black Lake.

I didn't know what I could do. I only knew I had to go to him. Or to her, to my mother, as she came to him. I couldn't tell how far away she was or how fast she came, but I knew she was coming in a whirl of wind and fire.

She came too fast for me. I ran and walked and ran and sat and walked again through the last of the dark and into the day and into the dark again, but I was just climbing the last hill before the pine valley when the brightness passed above me. The little stream blazed like a mirror in the sun, but it didn't rise up in steam. I had to squint my eyes against the light, but I didn't quite close them. The warmth was like standing near my uncle's forge, but it didn't hurt me. I felt and saw her passing, I called in my mind, but I didn't know whether I was more lonely or glad or afraid, or whether what I called was *Come* or *Go away*. Uncle Émon knew what he wanted. She went to him.

I shut my eyes and saw it all. He leaned against a tall boulder, tangled grass in front of him, empty air behind. His hands were empty. The cold breath of the lake on his back didn't warm when the rush of heat struck his face. The colors of the dry grass quickened to the hue of molten metal. Still Émon stood with his eyes open, calling *Anelé*! He held his arms out to her and stepped back into the empty air. I felt him falling through that wild light. I thought he was crying, and then I thought he was laughing, and then I thought there wasn't enough of him to do either—that inside him was only a hole that had been full of Anelé once and was now half full of what she had become and half of the cold lake-breath.

The lake reached him first. The heat fretted its smooth surface into a swirl of golden mist, but the dark and the cold were still there underneath; my uncle's body went numb as the water closed over him. He was still calling her, and she still came.

I saw the plunging fire. I saw the great golden

42

waterspout rising from the lake, whirling as high as the rock that my uncle had leaned on. Everyone who was awake in the Seven Villages saw the plume of steam cleaving the night. But the pain and the joy, the emptying and the filling…what really happened between my uncle and my mother…I know only a little of it in my blood, and none of it in my mind.

Later, as the grey light grew, I knew that he was still alive, cold and in pain and not caring enough to do anything about it. I didn't know whether I wanted to comfort or to punish him. To do either one I had to find him. I walked toward the lake, fighting blindly through the falling sheets of rain. It was coming down hard even for a Dragon-rain, but there was no gold in the huge hard drops.

I found him lying on his back at the edge of the lake, soaked and shivering, his skin blistered red. He turned his head toward me when I came close. His eyes frightened me. They were open but they didn't look straight at me, or at anything else I could see, and they were changed; not black any longer, but wild and golden. I saw that long before I understood that he was blind.

"It's me, Uncle Émon. Lirié. I came to take you home."

"There isn't any."

I helped him up and steadied him against my shoulder. I looked behind him to the Black Lake, which wasn't black any longer, nor so deep as it had been. It lay grey and empty under the grey sky.

I couldn't have gotten him home by myself. Aunt Lissé found us. She didn't ask what had happened; I guess she knew.

Nobody asked in Corlé either. When I told them they turned their heads away. Some folk from Lailé up the river came to look for the new burned ground, having taken the lake-steam for smoke, and I told them there wasn't any. After looking for days they decided I was right.

That was fifty years ago. We've learned to survive without the Dragon, if not to live. The first year we learned plowing and manuring, but we'd had the great rains to quicken the soil. The second year they waited a long time for the Dragon and the great rains to return, but at last they let Uncle Émon tell them what the trader had told him about irrigating. We raised enough food to live on, barely. For a while people sang the Dragon-songs. For a while we didn't sing at all. Now we sing work songs to keep ourselves going as we plow and weed and carry water, and little songs to keep ourselves company as we herd goats on the high slopes that are turning into desert. The children think that's life; it's all they've ever known. They stay away from Uncle Émon. They fear his intensity and pity his blindness. As I see the land's colors parching and paling with each passing year I envy what he sees, what he has seen these fifty years: Anelé coming to him in a shower of gold.

# The Call of Gold

*Claire Davon*

Humans died so easily.

The dragon circled the small castle, checking for survivors. To her satisfaction, nothing moved. The walls of the fortress where they had tried to fire arrows at her were black, char marks defacing the walls. Tumbled stones littered the area, victims of blunt attacks with her body. One of the turrets lay crumbled. Her wings spread wide across the sky, blotting out the sun. She circled again, saw nothing alive (that mattered) for miles, and descended. Bodies were strewn around the landscape, lying in heaps where she had destroyed them. They looked like broken dolls, and it wasn't until she got close enough that they resolved into the humans who had opposed her. They could not stop her now.

The scent was on the air, calling to her like a magic spell. The dragon dipped and wheeled, all thoughts of dead creatures vanished. There it was. Gold.

It winked at her, visible through the shattered roof, beckoning her. The humans had dug it out of her earth and then hoarded it, squirreling it away in goblets and coins, out of her sight, away from her use. It couldn't be allowed. It was hers. It was *hers.*

Gold. She had felt it inside the castle, through doors and locked away. It called to her, summoning her to this place. The color of her wings matched the objects. She raised her head, sniffed for a moment, and then lowered her head, diving to the places she scented metal.

Stones were no deterrent. Without humans to protect them the castle fortifications eventually gave, the stones yielding to her. Her wings battered them down, and her strong body cracked the mortar until it split apart. Chips flew around her until the formerly imposing walls and roof were in ruins, tumbling to the dirt in an arc. The castle would not be used for habitation again.

There it was. Her eyes whirled, refracting light. She folded her wings and landed, her feet making claw mark shapes in the dust of the building.

Gold.

Further evidence of the battle in singed bodies and dark walls was along her passage, but she paid it little attention. The gold was heaped in a room in the middle of the castle, in corners and on tables. The objects were tipped and scattered, disturbed by her ferocious attack.

Gold.

She reached the pile, and extended one wing. The wing had been battered in the violence, an open wound visible along the membrane. Her claw touched the gold first. She moved her wing slightly until the webbing lay alongside the precious metal. The mortar dust created a film over the air, like fog had descended.

She breathed in. Blood and fear smelled coppery, filling her nostrils with its odor. The odor of fire, her fire, and the tang of unburned stone, scorched but not damaged, was present. Later, in a day or so, the stench of decay would be present as the bodies strewn around the castle started their final journey to worms and earth.

The only aroma she cared about was that of the gold all around her. It called to her like a living thing. The membrane that stretched between her joints, giving her wing its strength, oozed blood. The tear had widened in her fierce battle with the stone and now the ooze turned to a steady drip drip drip.

Lifting her wing she touched it directly on one of the goblets, getting it as close to the torn membrane as she could. It had been convenient, for a time, to let humans dig her precious lifeblood out of the earth, until they had become greedy with it, and tried to withhold it from her. They could get to veins she couldn't reach. In some ways humans had advantages, despite their tiny size. They had hands that could lift and manipulate easily, hands she lacked. That was their only advantage.

The dragon sighed with relief when her wing touched the gold. Nothing happened for a moment and then slowly the goblet began melting into her wing. It appeared to flow up, the rim first settling into the membrane and then spreading out across more and more surface until the goblet had lost its shape and was a stream of gold flowing into the dragon. Torn flesh stopped oozing and as she watched. It knit back together until all that could be seen was smooth flesh.

The gold continued over her body, moving up her joints until it flowed into her scales. It fused with them, making each one it touched shine vividly. The contrasting scales around the new ones seemed pale and dark. Unlike silver, gold didn't lose its luster. The battle had coated her body with dirt and grime, darkening her in a way nothing else could. It was safer, she knew, not to gleam so brightly, but every fiber of her wanted to dip into the local pond and

49

emerge shining, her body glowing for all the world to see.

She rolled over, allowing the coins to sink into her scales. The smaller money vanished with a pop, melding into her body almost as soon as she touched them. The thicker ones were gone an instant later. The rest of the gold, like the goblet, took longer, flowing over her until they too merged with her scales and glowed on her hide.

Once all the gold had been absorbed, the dragon turned over again and got to her feet. She unfurled her repaired wings to their full length. In this small room they almost touched the walls. Gold gleamed in patches, the shiny bits showing where the new metal had become one with her flesh.

The dragon lifted her wing, admiring the new scales. She loved that she shone, unless she was dirty. She pitied her counterparts in silver and copper, who grew dull or green over time and had to renew themselves more frequently to stay shiny. There was nothing like the eternal shine of gold.

There was a hush over the countryside, but she knew it wouldn't last. Soon enough, riders would converge on the castle. As the days lengthened with no word from the fighters, reinforcements would be sent in to fill the gap.

The fill-in soldiers wouldn't know they were fighting a dragon, but it wouldn't take them long to discover the truth.

She stretched her wings again. They were whole, with no cuts along the membrane. Energy surged through her, feeding off the substance that gave her both her life and her color.

Man would come. She knew she could take them, but eventually they would overwhelm her, if she was capricious or unlucky. For now, she had what she had come for. Now it was time for repose. She would join her colleagues slumbering under the earth. Silver, bronze, copper and gold would rest wing to wing, dozing until it came time to rise again.

Rise, and feed. She had heard that gold gleamed off domes in land east of here. She was sated for now. But when she awoke again, she would visit these domes. Landing on them and sampling them would be…glorious. She would absorb their gleaming skins into hers, leaving behind the timber of a manmade object.

With that thought in her mind the dragon turned, and took to the air. Her wings carried her up and out of sight. Her resting place was far off, but the distance was nothing now that she was back at full strength. She was looking forward to seeing her compatriots again, deep in their cavern in the earth. Next time they woke, they would fly together and reclaim the metals that the humans had removed from the earth, and taken from them.

That day was coming. It would be glorious. Humans died so easily.

# Dragonfly Shadow
## A Dead West Tale
*J. Patrick Allen*

Amelia,

You once asked me about the incident in Navidad. I've searched long and hard in the steamer trunk of my mind for recollections, and the first thing that I always remember is the sight of a corpse basking on a river bank in August heat. Despite my young age I had seen far too many of these—but it was not a sight I was yet accustomed to. However, when I looked to Samuel there was none of the reaction I felt.

He did not appear to suffer from the burning of bile threatening to spill on the ground. His face was not green, no, his eyes hardly seemed to reflect anything other than a cool eye for details. This was not the first time he had seen things such as this. Samuel Henry Clayton had served in the war.

"Head's missing," was all I could croak. I was all of sixteen, and even with sickness strangling my vocal chords I still think I sounded too shrill, too young. I wouldn't feel comfortable with that voice until liquor, tobacco, and simple time altered the timbre.

Samuel knelt by the body, turning it with a lift of its shoulders. The body might have lain face down if it still had a face. "I can see that," he said without irony. "Heart's missing, too."

Nearby our horses whickered uncomfortably. Animals have keener senses than man and I believe they could sense something wrong in the air.

I pulled my handkerchief and covered my nose and mouth, fighting down my gag reflex. "What do you think? It's not bloated, but it might still have been a vampire case."

"Body's too new." My friend and mentor was my senior by twenty years, though experience could perhaps double that figure. He lifted the dead man's wrist and let it fall to the earth. It threw up a cloud of fine sand. "If this were a vampire slain and left out, it'd be more rotten than this."

"A little morbid for a run-of-the-mill prairie murder though, isn't it? It must be *some* kind of creature. We didn't get called out here for nothing."

He scratched at his jaw. "Could be. Doubt it. Get the mustard seed, would you boy?"

I jumped at the command, scrambling up the steep bank

to where his horse and my mule waited, swatting at flies. I searched through my packs and bags, filled with every possible sundry we could need. I laid hand on what I needed and trotted back to Samuel with a bottle bearing a white paper label marked *mustard seed*. You've not had to deal with such as vampires—of which I thank God every night when I pray—but the substance has a caustic effect on the creatures. It eats at their rotted skin and raises thick smoke like a sage fire. I heard a gentleman say it's a purifying substance like salt, and you know first hand what salt can do.

"Catch," I said, flinging the bottle. Samuel turned and caught it in a smooth motion, giving me the rude eye for throwing such a valuable resource.

He opened the flask and tipped some of the contents onto the bloody neck remnants. Yellow crushed powder sprinkled out and fell over the severed neck, down the back, and thickened in the blood.

"No reaction," he said pressing the cork back on. "Not a vampire."

"Victim, then?" I asked.

"Victim." Samuel stood, fanning himself with the brim of a hat that once upon a time had been a regal gray but which was now caked with so much dirt and layers of old sweat that it closer resembled black or brown in some spots.

"No bullet wounds," he said, scanning the area around us. I could tell what he was thinking—he was looking for places where such a man might be bushwhacked. "Lots of footprints. If I had my guess this is where the local congregation performs baptisms. Head taken clean off. No signs of tearing or sawing. Chest looks punched clean through to the heart."

Sensing what he was doing, I yanked out a small notebook and began jotting down what he was saying with the stub of an old pencil. "What does that mean?"

"Sharp instrument for the head, long. Expert work, and in one swipe. A good saber or cutlass could do the job if the man was capable enough. Spine's the only real trick to it." That was experience talking. "Chest could have been a knife. Hell, could have been claws. We close to town?"

I squinted one eye, trying to recall the map. "We're nearing the railroad, so we should just be a few miles off. We should be there by evening, but we could be there by afternoon."

He nodded, lost in thought. A buzzard's shadow swung

over us and that seemed to jolt Samuel out of his ruminations. "Afternoon, then. Let's do a quick search for the head. Doubt we'll find it."

"Anything listed in the Charlotte Bible that might do this?" I asked.

"Beheading *and* heart removal? Not that I know of." He glanced at me. "You know something?"

I shrugged, feeling uncomfortable under the weight of his stare. "Nothing for sure. Daniel Garner was telling me about them Aztecs and what-not. Said they sacrifice people like this."

"Daniel Garner says a lot of things," he said starting to move up the sand sculpted river bank. He cast his eyes back and forth for tracks, blood, anything. "More often than not, he's wrong. He prefers books to hunting."

I bit my tongue on the subject of Mister Garner. He was a fine member of our order, and more civil tongued than my mentor.

Say what one will about Samuel, though. His intuition usually proves right, and on the subject of finding this victim's head it was.

Navidad revealed itself a few miles on. A train must have

settled at the station as a big feather plume of steam rose against the Texas sky. A quarter mile outside of town a school house sat on a small rise overlooking the road into town and the Navidad River. A woman in blue stood beneath the branches of a tall old oak and waved goodbye to children leaving school. I knew none of those kids would be my age. Boys my age would be working full time with their fathers on one of the many family cattle or horse ranches out here.

"We're going to need to talk to the locals." It wasn't a question.

Samuel grunted in agreement.

"You gonna want a badge?" I asked.

"Most like." People tended to get itchy about folk asking about bodies unless they came with some kind of authority.

I leaned my head one way, then the other, thinking. "Ranger badge will probably be the best."

"When in Texas," Samuel said. "Pointless to use other badges hereabouts."

Navidad and the railroad faced off against each other from opposite sides of a broad dirt street. A hotel, some shops and saloons, a hossier, black smith. A decent spread of businesses faced out to the street with local houses

58

scattering on smaller lanes and alleys behind. We weren't in town long before I could tell why the townsfolk would hide behind their commerce. The smell coming off the stock yards in August was thick and sour, fully of musk and earth.

The town was busy. Men and women walked down the business side arm in arm, and workers (American and Mexican alike) crossed the street in front of us. A Friday afternoon, the local establishments would be preparing for the area farmers to come into town to do business and relax. And on top of that the train was loading cattle from the stock yards.

The shadow of a large cloud darkened the earth in front of us for a brief second and then it was gone.

The Paris Hotel was not quite as grand as its namesake. A two story wooden building, from counting the windows I surmised it probably had maybe ten rooms. It was squeezed in between the Feathered Lady saloon and a stable. We handed our horses in at the stable, paid for bed and board and took our bags next door.

Inside, the hotel smelled of new wood and fresh varnish. Brass oil lamps were fixed to either side of the grand stairway leading up to the rooms, and a small checkout

59

desk pocked with mail cubbies behind stood waiting our pleasure.

"Henry Clay," the man behind the counter said. He looked up at us, a briefly seen worry melting into a wide and warm grin. "You got my letter!"

"Robert MacLaine," Samuel said stepping up to greet the man with a firm handshake. "You're a long way off from Zanesville."

Robert MacLaine turned and gripped my hand in a firm shake. "Hello there Charlie, good to see you too. Well, Mister Clay, things got a little awkward after I nearly married that monster."

"Leanan sidhe," Samuel said. "Fairy creature. Probably not the original, or else she wouldn't have been so easy to kill."

"Yes, well, let a man use iron filings to melt your wife in front of the whole congregation and people start to look at you funny. After that I said to myself, 'Bob, it's about time you started that hotel you always talked about.' So's I found a quiet place where no one knew me to set up shop, and here I am."

"It's a fine establishment. Congratulations, Mister MacLaine."

"And," the proprietor said, reaching beneath the counter to present us with a key, "I've met someone."

"Have you now?" Samuel's eyebrow raised just a tick. I knew the real question in that sentence.

Apparently so did Mister MacLaine. "Oh yes. Her name is Margaret Ferguson, the local school teacher. And don't worry. She's human. Snuck some of those iron shavings into her soup over dinner one night. No reaction, except to scold me on my cooking."

Samuel took the key and tucked it in the pocket of his jacket. The circle and star of his Texas Rangers badge flashed from inside the jacket. He glanced around the empty lobby. "That's no guarantee, but still. You're almost certainly right. Any other guests staying the night?"

"None as yet, sir."

Samuel grunted and said, "So, tell me about these murders."

The proprietor licked his lips glancing at the doorway. Furtively, he gestured for us to follow him. He took us behind the counter, behind the wall with the mail slots, to his office. A handsome oak desk stood in the center of the room, piled upon with papers and leather bound ledgers. A large window behind it overlooked an alleyway lined with the doors of houses and lines of laundry hanging between.

He motioned for us to take a seat at the two wooden chairs facing the desk. He closed the door behind us and sat on the edge of the desk, wringing his hands.

"Our usual ordained authorities are concerned, and frankly I thought this sounded like it might be more in your domains. It started a few months ago," he began. "A man came through on one of the cattle drives. He was a vagrant, one of those men who wander from job to job—ah, no offense."

Samuel and I shared a glance.

"A-anyway. One morning the town woke up and found he was missing. His boss, wanting to see about hiring him for the next run, sent some men out to find him. He was outside of town, maybe a mile or so. Missing his ah—that is—his head and h-heart were gone."

I began taking notes.

Samuel's voice clicked into investigative mode, all warmth vanishing from it. "Where was it found?"

"A hill top, on Winslow Winchester's property. He was the one that found it. Said his cows usually prefer the hill top, but they were avoiding it that morning."

"And the head. Was it ever found?"

"No, sir."

I found myself mumbling, "That makes two at least."

Samuel gave me a sharp look and Mister MacLaine glanced in my direction.

"There's been another murder?" he asked.

Samuel glanced over my notes and nodded in approval before addressing Mister Maclaine. "Yes, sir. Found him on the way in. We may ask you to come out with us. Perhaps you can identify him. What can you tell us about the other deaths?"

Mister MacLaine tugged at his collar. "Well, one of the saloon workers followed after. They found him near a coyote den beside the railroad. Headless again. Uh, then John Gibson the horse rancher. This was inside his own home. Bachelor, so no one even noticed he was gone for several days. And then Gregory Kirkman."

"Where was he found?" I asked.

"Out behind the church. Someone during Sunday service noticed a smell. They've painted the spot over four times now and the blood always comes back."

*G. Kirkman—behind church,* I wrote down below the other murders.

"The first two, no names?" Samuel's hands lay perfectly

flat in his lap. He turned his head, looking at my notepad "Any patterns?"

"None I can see based on location alone. I mean, aside from the whole mess with the heads and hearts."

"And *none* of the heads have been found?" Samuel turned his gaze back on Mister MacLaine.

"None," he said with a certainty. "And no. The first two were migrant workers. I don't know their names."

"So this will make five deaths now," I said, closing my notebook. Outside the window, cloud shadows made alternating spots of dark and white roaming across the ground and houses. The light coming through the windows shifted color as the building fell into the shadow of an especially big cloud. The desk bell rang and Mister MacLaine shot to his feet.

"A visitor. Please excuse me." He hurried out of the office, leaving the door ajar.

Samuel nodded in my direction and then tilted his head toward the door. I nodded in understanding and got up, tucking the pencil and paper in my jacket pocket. With as much stealth as I could muster, I crept to the doorway and peered out, trying to remain unseen.

A Mexican man, tall and broad shouldered and with an

almost regal bearing stood at the desk offering an envelope to Mister MacLaine.

"Oh, Herman, thank you." MacLaine read off the envelope. "Oh, it's from Margaret. Thank you again!" The anticipation fairly quivered in his voice. He tucked the envelope in his jacket. The whole time Herman said nothing. He simply smiled and dismissed himself.

I was back in my seat by the time Mister MacLaine returned to the office. He waved the envelope, smiling.

"Sorry about that. One of the local boys came to deliver a letter from *her*."

Samuel's eyebrows raised appraisingly. "Her?"

"The woman I told you about. Her name is Margaret, and she's the local school teacher." He exhaled through his nose as he sat, looking satisfied. The envelope lingered near his nose as if he might pick up a hint of her smell on it. Realizing we were still in the room he opened a desk drawer to file the envelope away, but paused.

"Something wrong Mister MacLaine?" Samuel asked.

"The wax has been broken." He frowned at the envelope and then shook his head. "No, it's probably nothing."

Again Samuel and I glanced at each other. I shifted in my seat and asked the next thing at the tip of my head.

"The messenger seemed awful quiet. No hello or anything?"

"Oh, that was Herman." He waved a hand dismissively. "He moved her not long before I did. He's not quiet—he's mute. In his home town, wherever that was, someone removed his tongue."

Well that put a damper on the conversation.

"We won't keep you much longer." Samuel regarded the drawer Mister MacLaine tucked the envelope into. "Have there been any other strange occurrences?"

He tapped his chin. "We've had earthquakes the last few years. I honestly don't think much of them—they're relatively small and only happen once or twice a year. The old timers say they didn't used to happen, though. That useful?"

I could see that gave Samuel something to think about. He pushed up out of his chair and began for the door.

"Thank you, Mister MacLaine. Just one more question."

"Yes?" The proprietor was swiveling in his chair. I could tell already that letter was distracting him from the importance of our conversation.

"Have you told anyone else about our arrival?"

It took a second for MacLaine to react. "Well—just the

one. I've told Miss Margaret about you. Not what you do *specifically*, but that you were someone who could get to the bottom of what's happening."

I looked up at Samuel. He nodded, accepting the information but said nothing. He knocked on the door frame twice as we walked out already losing himself in deep thought.

We didn't leave the hotel before I had a forged Warrant of Authority for Samuel written up under the name James Butcher. And not before I'd done something about the dust on his wool coat and vest. I couldn't see that the shirt was cleaned—and it wasn't that Samuel cared. He'd step out in public completely red from dust if I weren't here. But if we were going to pose as authority figures, damnit, we'd look the part. I borrowed a rug beater from Mister MacLaine, and got rid of the worst of it before we were gone.

First part was introducing ourselves to the sheriff—one William Lovelace. He eyed the badge, but upon seeing the Warrant of Authority he settled down back down in his chair and popped the cork off of a bottle of scotch. Once established, Samuel acquired all the necessary details from the sheriff.

"I have my eyes on a few of the cattle drives. There are some boys that show up consistently around the time of the murders." Lovelace offered a finger of the scotch.

Accepting, Samuel raised the glass in thanks. "Any of them in town right now?"

"As you can see, the town's a little quiet right now. Which is to say, no."

He swirled the contents of the glass, watching the way the scotch clung to the sides. Samuel downed the tumbler and cleared his throat before saying, "Well, there's been another murder this morning."

He passed our details, including copies of my notes, to Lovelace and let him know where the body was. Lovelace was flabbergasted, stunned we didn't come to him first. Samuel said nothing as we walked out.

We asked around town. Anyone new showing up within the last six months? Well, no one regular, they'd say. Suspicious figures? Just them nacos who worked the stock yards or ranches. Occasionally some shifty folk from the cattle drives.

One man, a drunk, told us he knew where the heads were buried. He'd gladly show us if we'd buy him a drink. In full sight of the man the bartender shook his head.

"Don't listen to him, gentlemen. He's a chuckleheaded old fool."

The two of us returned to our rooms that night no more enlightened for our trouble. Watch schedule was arranged. Every two hours we switched, one of us in the rope framed bed, one of us in the rocking chair by the window with a loaded coach gun and a knife of cold iron.

Watches are hard work. The trick is to master the ability to remain clear headed and wide awake after a hard day of work and under the alluring effects of full dark trying to lull you to sleep. The chair was turned so I could see the window and our door at the same time, but the dark and the quiet always lulled me to sleep, if just for a minute or two. In one of those bouts, I may have heard the sound of the desk bell being rung. But if I did, my sleepy mind ignored it.

MacLaine was not around in the morning. The two of us dressed quietly, pulling on jackets over holsters weighed down by Colt army revolvers. His was a plain weapon, nondescript. The kind you might find in the hands of any law man or ex-soldier (despite his being on the wrong army in a past life). Mine had been purchased with my first real cut from a monster's bounty, and being prone to vanity as all young lads are, I had purchased antler grips and a finely tooled rig. Samuel disapproved, but he understood the urges of a boy and let me have it.

Finding the proprietor nowhere we stepped outside to find breakfast. Samuel patted his rumpled gray slouch hat back into shape and propped it on his head, watching the morning crowd. Saturday had arrived, and with it were carts and horses belonging to families from the outlying farms and ranches. The town buzzed with fresh life. I saw him chew his lip in thought.

"The crowd complicates things," I said, reading his thoughts. He merely grunted agreement and motioned for us to walk down the way to a small restaurant.

Breakfast was quick. The little establishment was full of people, but man who ran it—a portly fellow in a grease stained apron—found us a table in the corner and served us with hot coffee, beef brisket, and eggs. I wanted to stay for another cup of coffee, but Samuel slid a quarter under his plate and walked out as soon as he was done.

"What's going on?" I asked, following Samuel out of the restaurant.

"Crowd in the stock yard," he said gesturing with a tip

of his head. Surely enough, a pack of people had gathered one of the stockades which had been cleared of cattle. Between the movements of people I could catch snatches of Sheriff Lovelace. It was all men, that I could see. Women and children stood at the fences, the former trying to keep the latter from slipping past to look at what was happening.

People parted. Those that recognized us urged those that didn't to let us through.

Them who didn't catch the word saw the flash of tin at Samuel's breast. Lovelace looked a mixture of frustrated and relieved to see us. There, at Lovelace's feet, lay a headless body in dressing gown. The blood, what there was of it, soaked into the already damp mud of the stock yard, turning it a clay red.

He blew through his long mustaches and said, "I see my runner caught up with you."

"No sir," Samuel said. "We were having breakfast. I spied the commotion." He walked around the body until he stood opposite of me. "Who are we looking at?"

Lovelace blew through his mustache again. "Have you spoken to Robert MacLaine today?"

My throat tightened. Three years and I still wasn't used to this.

"This is him?" Samuel asked.

The sheriff nodded.

Samuel closed his eyes, giving a moment of silence. When he opened them all he said was, "He was a good man."

A cursory inspection was conducted, though Samuel found nothing illuminating. As before the cut was clean, done in a single stroke. And in and around the site there was no trace to be found of Robert MacLaine's head. The sheriff was already handling questioning, but I could see a different question forming in Samuel's eye. Before much more had gone on he excused himself.

"Come along, Charlie."

Samuel stormed the hotel and I followed. The place was in perfect order. The lobby, with its plush couches for smoking and visiting sat where they were. The front desk was arranged and ordered. I saw no sign of struggle. No claw marks. No scattered mess of destruction.

"What are we doing?" I followed just behind Samuel, but his legs were longer and his stride effortless.

Samuel rounded the desk and shoved open the door to the office. "Charlie, search his bedroom."

"Uh, yes sir. Are we looking for something?"

"I am. We're combing the site of the abduction."

Robert MacLaine's personal suite was not far from the office, located on the first floor. I rounded the corner of the hallway leading to it and stopped short. The door was open. Carefully, noiselessly, I drew my little hand cannon from its holster. Without even a breath, I thumbed back the hammer. The hammer's snap sounded like thunder in my ears. Would anyone be waiting for me there?

I took each step at an eternity, ensuring that there was not so much of a tap of leather on wood, not so much as a creak from the floor boards. Silent as deer stalking, I poked my head in the door, gun drawn and ready.

It was empty.

With equal caution I entered and walked to the wardrobe. I flung it open, ready for someone to leap out at me. There was nothing but wool suits and the smell of mothballs. I released a tensed breath that had coiled in my chest like a spring. More bravely, I checked beneath the bed. Again, there were no bogeymen waiting for me.

The bed was unmade. A corner of the sheet and blanket were tossed aside as if its previous occupant had risen suddenly with an urge to piss but the chamber pot was empty on that account. A further search of the bedroom revealed nothing elucidating. If MacLaine left this room, it was of his own will.

"We're leaving."

I nearly jumped out of my skin. Spinning, Samuel was there, an envelope in his hand.

"God in heaven, Samuel!"

His brows raised.

"I kept expecting his murderer to be waiting for me."

"Good instinct, but the place is empty. Finish up. We're leaving."

"Did you find anything?"

He held up the envelope. "Found this. Remembered Mister MacLaine has a lady friend."

I gave the room one last look-over, my heart galloping in my chest. And then we left.

On the way out something glinting in the morning light caught my eye. Near the desk. I paused, bending over to pick it up. It was a feather, like a bird's, but in a scintillating array of colors. It dazzled and sparkled in the shaft of yellow light pouring through the windows, looking more metallic than natural.

"Samuel," I said, looking up.

He paused, looking at the feather I held in my hand. His mouth was a hard line. He came forward and I passed it to him. Samuel gave it a turning inspection, checking it from every angle.

"No Texas bird would drop these."

"Parrot, maybe?"

"Too large…"

"A peacock, then? I read in a book they have colorful feathers."

Samuel shook his head. "Too small by far." He tucked the feather in his breast pocket. "Come along. We have someplace to be."


There was a small house beneath a mesquite tree between town and the steepled school house. This was where Margaret Opal Ferguson, beloved of school children and hotel proprietors, lived. Tall yellow prairie grass crept all the way up to the picket fence—which was just shy of needing a new coat of white wash—but ended its march there. Beyond that was a beautiful green lawn with flag stones leading up to the covered porch.

We hitched our animals at the picket fence, letting them dine on the prairie grass, and let ourselves in the gate. At two knocks on the front door we heard foot steps and the woman I'd seen the previous day opened the door.

"Hello, can I help you?" She was lovely. Perhaps only a few years older than myself. Margaret's flyaway curly hair was put up in a bun, and she wore a fashionable, if modest, dress. She would have blended into of the parlors of the wealthy in Washington or Chicago. She was lovely.

Samuel held up the envelope, his face grim. He always knew how to make an impression. "Miss Ferguson, my name is Henry Clay. This is Charlie Kirchner. May we ask you a few questions?"

Recognition bloomed. "O-of course. Come in. Robert told me about you."

"He mentioned something along the lines to us, in passing." I tried to give her a reassuring smile, but she looked worried.

She bit her lip and led us into the humble, if well appointed, sitting room. "Have you spoken to Robert?"

I opened my mouth, but Samuel beat me to it.

"Miss Ferguson, Robert was found dead this morning."

Margaret nodded silently, biting her lip. "I had a feeling. Last night—I had a terrible premonition. Gentlemen, are you superstitious?"

Samuel and I paused halfway to sitting down on her couch. We glanced at one another.

"We keep open minds," he said.

"I woke in the middle of the night. The sky around my house was starless, as if something directly above blocked the sky. And I knew—I just had a *feeling* that something terrible had happened." Sniffled into a handkerchief. "And I fear it was my fault."

Margaret tried to keep her composure. She sat in a cane-bottom chair, adjusting her skirts. But her hands were shaking and I could see the blood drained from her face.

"Why do you think it was your fault?" I asked. My heart leapt for her. I wanted to go to her, put my arm around her and stroke her hair. I wanted to tell her everything was all right. I wanted to kill the bastard that threatened her.

She looked between the two of us. Her eyes were scared, haunted. In mere moments, deep circles had formed beneath them. She studied Samuel's badge and my face before speaking. "Robert had just begun to court me, and well… People who love me have a horrible tendency to die."

"A tendency to die *could* be considered horrible in most circles," Samuel said with a twist of his lips. I kicked his shin with the heel of my boot.

"You don't understand. My parents—they were missionaries. When I was a child we were sent by our congregation to Uman, Mexico. There, they died of a Malaria which nearly took me. I survived, but just."

I began to scribble notes. *Uman, malaria, parents deceased.*

"By God's grace I was adopted by my uncle and aunt in Alton, Illinois."

"I know the place," Samuel said. We'd hunted a gigantic man-eating bird there two years back. It lived in a series of caves on the Mississippi.

"My uncle was terribly fond of me, but on a trip to St. Louis he was killed helping a Freedman. I fear my aunt only survived me because after his death she bore love for no one, much less myself."

"And I'm assuming she's alive?" he asked.

She nodded, a nervous jerky motion.

"Well go on, woman," Samuel said.

She hesitated, her voice momentarily gone. Finding it, she said, "A man cornered me, not too long ago. He was from a cattle drive, and clearly drunk. He—he tried to have his way with me. I was rescued by Robert and my dear friend Herman. They stayed with me the rest of the night to make sure I was safe, but the next day the man was found. W-with no huh-head." She swallowed a sob. "So many other men have experienced the same! Men who gave me flowers, men who stopped to talk to me, even a man who simply looked my way. Is that how they found sweet Robert?"

I looked down. There were no words.

Margaret began crying in earnest. There would be getting no further story from her until this storm subsided. I pushed off the couch and walked to the kitchen. A pail of milk sat on the counter, apparently being prepared for butter churning before our arrival. I took a ladle and poured a glass for her.

Samuel joined me there, leaning in close. "So, five men dead and likely connected to the school teacher."

"You don't honestly think she did it, do you? *Look* at her."

He laid a hand on my shoulder. His tone was regretful. "You said the same thing about that witch in that logging camp."

"In Minnesota? She wasn't *innocent* but she *had* been defending herself!"

"That may be the case here, but if she's up and ripping out hearts, beheading men…" His gaze was distant, looking out the window without seeing. "No, I don't think she's doing it. I think there's something else. Had Robert still been alive, had I not known him, I would guess he was the culprit."

I walked the cup of milk back to the living room and gave it to her, making sure she drank every drop. We were finished with our questioning, but Samuel wanted to make sure things were as he suspected.

"Mind if I take a look around?" he asked.

Margaret gave her consent and Samuel asked me to stay with her to make sure she was alright. When he passed he leaned in muttering, "You're better at this socialization mess than I am."

He searched the property—looking for piles of severed heads, I supposed—and I sat at the kitchen table watching Margaret go about cooking.

"This was supposed to be supper for Mister MacLaine and I. I was to have him over," she said. As if picking at a scab, the crying began again. This happened several times during Samuel's search.

During a calm moment I pulled out the feather and

watched the way the waning afternoon light played against its metallic tines.

"Like a bird of paradise," I said to myself.

"Hm?" Margaret looked over her shoulder. "Mister Kirchner!"

I looked up. "Yes, ma'am?"

She swept across the small kitchen and snatched the feather from my fingers. "I do not know how you were raised, but where I come from it is considered impolite to take things from a person's belongings!"

"What—no—!" I threw my hands up, as dismayed as surprised.

The door opened and Samuel entered, surveying the scene. The school teacher was red-eyed, the feather in hand, her lips squeezed tight in indignance. He eyed the feather.

"I think there may be a misunderstanding here," was all he said.


Supper was lamb stew with carrots and green beans and potatoes fresh from the garden out back. Each of us took up a fresh cup of milk with our meals and broke hot bread. The food was savory and chewy. Everything was heaven. I might have shoveled food into my face with both hands had I two spoons.

Sullen as always, though, Samuel sat across from Miss Ferguson. Between the two of them lay two nearly identical feathers. Both of the same size, the same coloration. The only difference was age. On the left we had today's feather, found on the floor of the Paris Hotel. On the right we had Miss Ferguson's feather, slightly faded in age though still beautiful.

"In Mexico?" I said between bites of stew-soaked bread heel.

"In Mexico," she said tapping the feather. "There was a local orphan boy. He was my age, and we used to play together, and often I would relate the lessons I'd learned from my parents to him. He stayed at my side while I was sick unto death. When I was bound to leave he came to me and gave me this feather."

That was something to think about. I jotted down notes on the feather and its origin. "Have you seen this boy again?"

She shook her head. "He was just an orphan child in Uman. I wonder about him often, but I doubt I'd see him again unless I returned."

Throughout the meal Samuel continued to stare at the feather. Occasionally I'd hear him mutter the word 'Mexico' over and over again. That was the key, then. What ever protection Miss Ferguson received, it began in Mexico.

"There's nothing in the Charlotte Bible comes from Mexico," I said quietly, earning a curious look from Miss Ferguson.

"I know," Samuel tore a chunk of bread stuffed it into his mouth. "Heard a legend somewhere, but I'm trying to recall it. P'raps it was that Aztec mess you mentioned."

When supper was ended, I helped Miss Ferguson clean up. Samuel had the Charlotte Bible now, and was flipping through the pages for anything that might help. This book, as you know, is the collected knowledge of all the men in our fraternity and there was nothing in the book as yet to warn us of what was to come.

I could hear a nasal huff—all I needed to know the search was not going well.

"Might not strictly be from Mexico." I was elbow deep in water, scrubbing off dishes. "We hunt plenty of things out here that aren't *from* here. Maybe who ever is at the root of all this was a transplant to Mexico like Miss

Ferguson here."

She glanced between the two of us, her mouth slightly open as if she were about to say something. It seemed she was entirely unsure of what to make of our conversation.

Samuel snapped the over-full book shut and pushed away from the table. "We need to lure the killer out."

Miss Ferguson swallowed, her hand faltering on drying a plate. "How would we do that?"

His eyes shifted from the floor, to her, and back. "We need to put you in danger. Make it—him—think we aim to harm you."

"Absolutely not!" Before I knew it I was shouting. "We will not hurt her."

"Charlie…" he began.

"No. No innocents. We put ourselves in danger, but we're not putting her out there."

He studied me for a moment. Finally he nodded slowly and fell back into his chair, pulling out a tobacco pouch and pipe from his jacket. "You're right, of course."

We fell to silence again. I scrubbed, Miss Ferguson washed, and Samuel puffed away at his pipe lost in the myriad worlds of thought. I still felt burned that Samuel would even think of such an option. But then—well, then it hit me.

"We don't have to put her in danger," I said, turning back to him.

"How do you—oh, you sly dog." He stood again, grinning smoke. "Of course. Mister MacLaine was no danger to her. He was a suitor."

"Yes. Yes! This thing, what ever it is. The killer *loves* her."

Miss Ferguson's breath caught. For a moment I thought we might have torn the scab off all over again. But she nodded. "We must endeavor to make him jealous, then. For Robert's sake, as well as my own." She laid a hand on my arm and I could feel the blood rush to my cheeks. "Would you help me?"

Words failed me. Samuel watched, amused, as I tried to form a sentence. At last I gave up and nodded.

Plenty of folks were still in town the next afternoon. Once the churches let out families would stick around for a meal at one of the restaurants, or to talk out business with neighbors. Thick cotton mountains crossed the blue afternoon sky, traveling quickly under a wind far stronger than what we felt on the ground. Miss Ferguson walked by my side, held my arm, stopped periodically to kiss my cheek. And of course, people watched. It was common knowledge that Miss Ferguson and the late Mister MacLaine were fond of each other, and now here she was on the arm of a stranger and he not even in the ground yet. She did her best to look the part of someone in love, but I could tell by the way her nails dug into my arm that the stares hurt.

Samuel was somewhere—always somewhere—out of sight. He agreed to stalk us, to wait and watch. Our intention was to gauge the reactions of the townsfolk and find the person most hurt by Miss Ferguson's play at affection.

She spied someone. "Oh, here darling. Herman. Herman!" She waved an arm to the Mexican worker, the man who had delivered the envelope. He stopped mid stride and peered at us. Cloud shadows crossed the road, at a steady clip, but the one covering him stopped as well.

And that was when I began to pay attention.

He eyed us, then crossed closer. There was a mask of suspicion, but I saw him cleverly hide it. He came close, all congenial smiles for Miss Ferguson. That shadow, massive, curling, *long*, followed him. I watched it, studied the shape of it and looked up. There was no corresponding cloud that could account for that immense shape. And as I studied the shape I began to reckon what it was. It was as a cross, where the arms of the cross corresponded to wings. Damn me, but it looked like a dragonfly.

"Herman, darling." She curtsied to him as he came close and he kissed her hand. All his noble bearing was present. A long regal nose, a kingly gaze. This man didn't look like a humble mute farmhand. He didn't look like the sort of man who had been beaten down by the kinds of abuses that Texan ranchers gave to Mexican workers. This man looked like a king.

"Herman, I want to introduce you to my fiancée. His name is Charlie Kirchner. Charlie, this is Herman. He's a dear friend. He arrived in Navidad shortly after I did, and he's been here to help me on so many occasions. He's a darling, I assure you."

The mute and I shook hands, appraising each other. It was the age old dance between two men courting the same woman. The glances, the grip of the hands, the tensing of muscles—all the jigs and reels a mischievous God built into man from the days of Adam.

"I get the impression your name is not actually

Herman," I said. Daniel Garner's old stories came back to me.

He inclined his head, and Miss Ferguson turned to me about to ask me a question.

"No," I said. "It's Hernan, isn't it?"

Then he smiled and tipped his head just so. And through our gripped hands he gave me a vision. It struck like lightning, electrified me. He wasn't a migrant worker. He was a mighty Aztec or Mayan king. A mighty Mesoamerican god. I saw past the man in the dirty broad cloth shirt. I saw him in his ceremonial garb, bare chested, crested in a gold head piece. And I saw past *that* to the creature beyond. And it was immense.

Spanning over the town of Navidad, writhing in the sky as it drifted aloft the currents of the wind, was an immense and sparkling snake. It dwarfed the small railroad town, breathing lightning and flapping its ancient rainbow-feathered wings. Each scale looked like it had been carved from a different metal, each one was a knife of silver or gold or iron. And it stared down at me, and bared its wicked fangs in a grin that I did not like at all.

My voice left me. Left me as surely as it had been robbed of Hernan. I pulled away from the ancient serpent god, pulled away from Miss Ferguson. Hernan smiled, dipping a bow, and left us.

Miss Ferguson, Jesus bless her, pulled me aside. "Charlie, you're shaking!"

"Him," I stammered. "He's the one. I know what he is."

I let her pull me deep into the evening shadow of a gap between buildings. There Samuel was already waiting for us, a long barreled buffalo rifle in hand. We explained to him what happened. I explained what I saw. I knew better than to expect shock, surprise on that steady face. Samuel considered my words.

"They're all over Mexico," I said. "Not the creatures, but carvings of the creatures—creature. That may be *him*. He's name begins with a Q." I snapped my fingers. "Quitz-quetz- ketz—"

"Who told you all this?" he asked.

"Daniel Garner, at the Charlotte conference two years back. Said he doubted they existed, but you know how he is."

"They *what?*" Samuel raised a hand to smack me.

"Some kind of serpent god, Samuel. A great big feathered snake! Daniel said when Hernan Cortez first arrived in Mexico City they thought he was this god of theirs come to walk the earth."

He scratched as his jaw, considering. "Collects everything, even if he's not sure it's real." Despite the number of times Garner's contributions to the Charlotte Bible had saved our hides Samuel often complained of the size the book had grown to.

"If witches, ghosts, and demons exist, then anything can."

He snorted. "So we're talking to this Hernan Cortez?"

"Hell if I know, Samuel. Maybe this god has a sense of humor and decided he liked the name. What ever it is, I remember Daniel saying one of the god's domains was knowledge."

Samuel looked to Miss Ferguson, who by now was peering at us as though we'd sprouted wings. "Fits the profile, then. This thing has a sweet spot for the school teacher who spent time in Mexico."

"What in heaven's name—?" She had backed up by now, holding up her hands. "I surely do not know what you two are on about."

I was the one to intervene. Samuel left all issues of tact in my hands. "Miss Ferguson, we… Samuel and I—"

"Herman—his name is Herman—surely can't be any

kind of murderer much less a monster. He's a harmless ranch hand."

"Samuel and I, we're not…" We're not officers is never a good way to start a conversation. "We don't deal specifically with human murders. We—well, our specialty is *in*human issues. Mister MacLaine probably didn't explain all this, but we helped him ages past. It was a fairy—it was trying to feed off of him."

Her spine went stiff at the proprietor's name. "Robert would say no such thing. He is a man of senses."

"Precisely, which is why he recognized what was wrong. Please, ma'am. We're just here to help."

"Well you can help without me. I will not be part of your scheme." And with a sharp jab of her chin into the air, she spun and walked out on us.

Samuel's hands rested tight on the barrel of the buffalo rifle. I saw the tense set of his jaw.

"I don't think she'll tell the sheriff." I wasn't as sure of that as I wanted to be.

"It's time we lit out. Found ourselves a new camp."

"What about Hernan?"

"We still have our bait. It's all we need."

"What do you mean?"

He strode past me, slinging the rifle over his shoulder. "Wants you next, don't he?"

Preparation is hard when you don't know the particulars of what you're hunting. With demons you can use scriptures and holy water. Vampires are not fond of garlic or mustard. If you can take away a witch's book then she's as good as lost, and even the smartest troll usually falls for basic hunting traps. But what do you do about a god? Would he walk up to us? Would he fly? Would he strike us afar with that lightning?

We did the best we could with limited supplies. Guns were loaded and left out where one was always in reach. Samuel helped me dig and stake shallow tiger pits, and I added a few scattered about in case he had a careless step before that. But hell, we were lost on what to do beyond that. Wasn't the first time, and you know it wasn't the last.

We didn't start to cook supper until the sun was well biting into the horizon. It consisted of stale bread and a couple slabs of steak fried over an open fire and washed down with a few swallows from a bottle of cheap bourbon. Samuel made no show of hiding us out on the prairie beside the river. The fire was built on stones pulled from the river well away from any tree stands, and he made sure it was a nice and smoky one. Anyone riding out here at night would see us from miles off.

The stars began to come out and our Mexican friend didn't interrupt dinner, so we relaxed back on our bedrolls. Entertainment was the kind of limited conversation I always got out of Samuel, accompanied by a show of him trying to pick the stringy tough beef out of his teeth with a knife.

I tried to collect my thoughts, recalling everything I'd learned from Daniel at the last meeting of our order, the Knights of Charlotte.

"His dumbness," I said. "There's an old legend that Quitz—uh, Quetzalcoatl tried to fly up to the sun and the sun punished him for his pride by removing his tongue. The serpent has a sister that raised him somewhere out there, and occasionally he quakes the earth so that she knows he's alright."

"That explains the earth quakes. Better than a telegraph." With a jerk of his head, he let his hat fall into his face. I knew better than to think he was asleep. Samuel's ears were as sharp as anyone's. He was listening.

I sat late into the night. My revolver lay close at hand, but it was the Enfield rifle in my lap that brought me the most comfort. The old buffalo rifle wouldn't do us much good—it was too dark to see that far. But this boy, well… It was Samuel's gun in the war, but I'd used it to fell the first creature that ever tried to kill me. It was lucky. It was *mine*.

It wasn't until I heard the distant drumbeats of thunder that I realized the stars were gone. Night had fallen long since, and our conversation had died away hours ago. Samuel still lay with his hat over his head, but I watched him thumb back the hammer of his Colt.

Wind began to whistle across the grass, canting the brush to one side as though the world itself had been tipped just so. And as that wind came, it carried with it the muttered sound of thunder rippling closer. I pulled back the hammer on the old percussion rifle and double-checked to make sure my Colt was ready.

There wasn't the sound of crunching footsteps over summer-dried grass. Nor the sound of wings flapping in the wind. It was a silent thing that came over us. The camp fell into deadly quiet, no wind stirring and the thunder utterly absent. Even the sound of the river became dead to us. And there I saw him.

With visible approach he appeared at the edge of the camp. I leveled the Enfield and snapped off a shot. There was the snap of the hammer hitting home, and the deafening crack of the powder igniting. Smoke and light exploded into the coal-dimmed ring around our camp. Hernan was not stirred.

In that instant I realized that his human shape was half-formed. The night was not concealing him. Rather I could see the night *through* him. Instinct drew my eyes up, and there against the flashing thunderheads I saw the serpent waving like a banner in the wind.

Its wings caressed the sky, gently keeping it aloft. It regarded me with viper eyes. Black powder thunder split the air again, and more smoke filled the area. Samuel, unseen, had drawn his revolver and pointed it at the Serpent's maw.

He fired.

To no effect. The serpent god was not stirred by our arms. It dove through the sky, lanced downward, over our traps. The mouth opened, the fangs were bared, and flashes of lightning rose in its throat.

"Herman?" A voice called.

Miss Ferguson rose out of the dark, stunned. Her eyes

lay on the serpent, and its gaze met hers. I could see the creature twitch. It tried to redirect the strike, but too late.

I'm not sure of the specifics of how it appeared to others, but I can tell you that the lightning strike came to me as immense heat. There was a vague buzz in the air about me, and the world turned luminous and blue. There was fire, and there was heat.

As Samuel tells me, he screamed and unloaded the rest of his revolver onto the creature. Miss Ferguson stumbled past our pits and fell to me, frightened by what she saw in the sky. Later she would tell me she had only come to us to apologize.

The serpent vanished amidst Samuel's volley and Hernan stepped into the ring of light fully tangible. I think he sought Miss Ferguson's gaze, her understanding. He earned her gaze, but what he must have seen there—what I can only imagine he found—was fear. Samuel says Hernan opened his tongueless mouth as if to say something, his eyes ever on Miss Ferguson. He must surely have not seen what Samuel did next.

Samuel pulled his old cavalry saber to hand, and with a mighty swing he severed Hernan's head cleanly from the neck. The spine gave him no trouble. Whether this is the proper way to kill a god, I do not know, but it was the way Hernan sacrificed his enemies. Hernan fell to the dirt and the night fell quiet. The serpent was not to be seen again— not that we heard at least.

In the morning the feathers covered the town and country for miles around. Rainbow feathers strewn far and wide, scattered by the night's wind. What little energy was left in the storm after he died must have spread them across the whole of the county.

I woke later. In the next week I was tended by a local doctor for lightning strike. I was out of bed and walking shortly though I would be stiff for a while yet. Thankfully the blow was indirect, and therefore was not fatal.

Miss Ferguson was thankful that we were there to avenge Mister MacLaine's death, but her thanks was a cold thanks. Samuel and I, we were long since used to such thanks. Looking back, she'd lost too much in too short a time. A lover, a good friend, her reputation, and a sense of what the world is.

Our only payment was a meal packed for the road and a rather impressive looking scar. We passed by her house before we left to say goodbyes. I insisted. She kept her distance with me, but I could see it was her way of mourning. By the looks of the wagon in her yard she was fixing to leave just like us. After a refused offer of help we left her to her packing. We were busy men in those days.

We had places to be.

# Dreaming of Dragon Wings

*T. Fox Dunham*

Amber darted through the concrete chunks, these sculptures dedicated to decay—gravestones marking the passing of the old cities. She hid below a bridge, dodging the shadow tendrils. The young warrior tasted ozone, and her hair sparked from the energy of the techno-spirit. Where did the shadows keep their slaves? They were still human, even though their minds had been hollowed out. The mind always kept the young ones alive, fed them, using them for its labor force. Amber's sister still had to be alive. The chaos of the crushed and fallen city sprawled out as far as she could see. Old buildings fell. Roads cracked. Metal poles rusted, and metal skeletons decayed along the avenues. The possessing dragon showed her the routes, casting visions to her mind, maps of the city. She didn't know how the dragon spirit knew the way, but she trusted it, knowing it well. It was a part of her.

Amber sensed the fear of the young dragon spirit—an untried warrior. Both of them had become kin when the elemental imbued her body, found perch in her heart. She also sensed its blame. The dragon accused humans for the destruction of the natural world. She felt the dragon's judgment, but it was the right of such old creatures to convict humankind for the darkness they'd created in their search for paradise. She'd heard legends of the marvels made in machine, the powers that had been woven from metal—minds in boxes and mouths that could be carried to send a voice across the planet. The foolish generation that came before sent men and woman to other stars and down to the bottom of the sea. Amber thought of the wonders, and her partner sent another vision: a giant mouth devouring, eating spirits and then consuming the skies. Clouds like mushrooms erupted into the horizon, burning men women and children. The forests died. The earth wept red rain. "My generation did not destroy the world," she whispered. "We did not spew this poison on the earth. But I do feel some responsibility. We will learn." It felt hope, and Amber believed that her kind might be redeemed.

Amber fetched her bow from her back, prepared an arrow, but she knew it wouldn't be of use. The shadows, like their namesakes, bore no physical form. They drove their fingers into flesh and ripped the spirit out of the body. Then it possessed you, but not like the dragon spirits who had awakened when the world began to die. The demons of lost technology enslaved your mind and controlled you like a puppet, serving to maintain the machine. Amber scanned the horizon from her hiding place. Great pillars rose into the sky, pouring smoke. Smog congested the old ruins. Lights flared through the mist, blinking from the center of their webs. Hordes of the taken serviced the machines, fueled into the furnaces, oiled gears and served food of the spirit to the shadows. Lanna was one of the multitudes—her sister caught in the web. Amber had to hope that she could be brought home, that some part of her soul survived and was just imprisoned, suppressed by the shadow machines. If taken care enough away from the source, perhaps she could be restored to Amber's family.

The ground shook. Dirt shifted. Concrete bits vibrated than rolled out of the way. Metallic tendrils broke through the ground, reaching out of debris. Amber dodged out of their way, and the claws raked the earth, striking for the young warrior. She ran for cover, to get out of their obvious range. She aimed her bow and fired an arrow. The simple weapon flew then struck an armored plate. Steel scales made up the creature's skin, and Amber suspected this was just the arm of the terrible beast. She aimed again, this time for the thin spaces between the armor. Her dragon spirit passenger showed her a vision of moonlight than still water, calming her, aiding in her concentration. Amber hoped that eventually it would be able to do more than offer advice through daydreams. She shot again, and the arrow struck the beast's soft underbelly. It screamed, slashing in the air with its slender fingers. Quakes shifted the landscape. The body must have stretched out for miles, rooted into the old city, dug down into the earth . . . waiting.

Amber darted forward. The dragon showed Amber a vision of a broken sundial. The stone chronometer had broken, fallen off a pillar. Its gnomon cast an imprecise shadow, marking the wrong time. "I have to find her." The dragon growled in her chest, shaking her body, nearly throwing her off her feet. Its opposition nearly petrified her. The metal snake recuperated, renewing its control. She had to move now. "We're coming back." Finally, the dragon relented, and she ran back along the path, heading for the border forests and cover. The shadows never left the city. At least, that's what her tribe believed.

They gathered their human slaves, and the humans could leave the hive. The shadows sent them to attack the tribal villages, abducting more flesh to serve the furnace. This is how they came in the night and stole Lanna away. She was close. The dragon spirit empowered her eyes to see and hear further. Her sister languished, asleep, and called to Amber in dreams.

Amber ran from the city, afraid and defeated by the metal beast. She needed greater strength and skill to break through their defenses. She had avoided the training dragon elders, even though her grandmother had compelled to seek out the old woman of the mountains, the only teacher in range. Amber promised her grandmother she would find her, to become all she could be, to walk in legend, but Amber had avoided seeing the elder. She feared the fury unleashed. Many who carried the spirit maddened, going insane and ripping apart their own bodies to tear out the power. It burned in them like a sun, destroying them.

But it was time. Understanding the power, using it was the only way she could bring Lanna home.

Amber left her village at dawn and climbed the cliff at first light. Her hands ached by the time she reached the outcropping, following a natural chimney, tracing the scent of burning wood and smoke. A gentle melody sung from the top. A crone hung over a modest fire. Flowered robes wrapped around her shoulders, covering her head and eyes. She leaned on a knobby staff, and gazed into the licking flames. Amber adjusted the bow hung on her back and pulled down her leather skirt, trying to look dignified, worthy.

"At last, the child spirit is born," the elder said.

"I was born eighteen seasons ago."

"The other child," the elder said. "The boy. A wild one there. Could be your fierce friend, a good ally or a petulant child struggling to take control, sure of his own wisdom. Yet both of you are in need of guidance, training. Come sit with me by the fire." Amber sat on a flat stone. Winds whipped the side of the eastern mountains, chilling her to her bones, and she wrapped the fox furs tighter around her neck and vest. She warmed her hands. "Are you a coward?"

"My grandmother says I'm very brave," Amber responded, worried she'd be caught in a lie. What could the elder see?

The elder inhaled, paused in silence then exhaled. "Yet you live in shame."

"I failed my sister."

"And you live to try again. The spirit in you knows patience, though it has its own rage. It struggles also,

104

fighting the forces you have given it in symbiosis. Which nature will dominate?"

"Sometimes the visions inflame my mind," Amber said, suddenly exhausted from the climb and from carrying this heavy spirit, too great for her meek body.

"Either you will learn to live in balance with your little brother dragon or you will burn in madness. If your mind endures, your heart will not."

Tears wet Amber's eyes. She calmed herself, remembering her warrior's strength. Her grandmother had been a wise hunter in the clan, and she had taught Amber to focus. "How do we begin?"

"When did the dragon spirit first commune with you?"

"A season ago. I gathered mushrooms among the roots of an ancient oak in the forest outside of my family's camp while hunting boar. I gathered food for my grandmother to make the midday meal for my family while my mother tended to my younger brothers and sisters. I tripped and fell into the roots, down into darkness like caves carved into the base of the tree. The dragon had slept there for many centuries, and it had awoken. Dragons had awoken from hibernation and come back to our world. I breathed it in, taking deep the mist, the spirit. The fire burned my blood.

Then dragon spirit showed me such beauty—and the darkness of our kind. It showed me what we did to the natural world and how what we humans had created came alive then moved over the earth like a shadow."

The elder picked up a clay pot from crimson coals and poured her a cup of tea. Amber sipped it, and at first the pungent flavored stirred her tongue. She nearly spit it out but didn't wish to be rude.

A vision overwhelmed her mind: a groundhog running away from a porcupine flooded Amber's mind. The dragon spirit filling Amber called her a coward. Amber still couldn't get used to the power of the waking dreams the dragon spirit employed, taking over her brain. She didn't quite understand the vision. Sometimes, she had to contemplate on the essence of the cryptic images before knowing the young spirit's intentions. She sighed then sipped the tea again, this time with an open mind and pallet. She tasted the bitter flavor, the flowery scent and let her mouth get comfortable with the elder's tea.

"The young dragon of trees speaks to you now? Shows you visions? Yes?" The elder set the pot back into the coals to keep the water hot then sat next to Amber on the mossy stones—the old woman of medicine and moons. Hawks soared overhead, gliding along the edge of the mountain. They opened their wings wide and sailed through the air, circling above the mountain's edge. The dragon spirit stirred in Amber's chest, filling up her body, pressing into her limbs. Her flesh felt like it expanded, ready to burst like a water skin left in the rain. The dragon watched the hawks through Amber then shouted visions of flight into her head. Her body ached with the need to take the air, to know the wind, to ride like a mount. She nearly leaped from the mountain but grabbed a granite chunk, holding on in case she lost control. The spirit grew roots into her chest. Warmth suffused through her skull. Green light shined on the ground, emitting from her eyes.

"I can't always control it," Amber said. "I want to jump off this cliff and fly into the sun."

"You have no wings."

"I want to hunt at the running animals and pick them up into the air." The spirit possessed Amber, compelling her words. She lost herself, drowned in the overwhelming elemental.

"But you have no talons."

"I need to weep for all the pain this world has suffered while I have slept."

"And that is your burden," the elder condemned, but she offered her gnarled hand in comfort. Amber enlaced her fingers with the old twigs. "Now calm the elemental force that holds you. Do not fight it but let it flow."

"But I will jump!" she said, gripping the elder's hand, holding onto for life. The dragon compelled her to leap and fly. She had no wings—not yet. She had not yet become.

"Tell your companion it must be patient. You are both young and require time to bond."

"It will not listen!" She tried to concentrate, to draw her from her patience as a warrior, but it struggled. She remembered the hunt, the way she waited in the forest, not hiding but merging with the trees, flowing like a leaf on the breeze. She didn't need to be silent but simply to be, exist and merge into the music of the woods and wait for the deer to walk into view. She'd aim her bow. The tendon flexed with her tendons, moving to the forest beat—slow, ever so slow and careful.

"I see the calm in your eyes," the elder said.

"I am thinking of hunting."

"Now show those memories to the spirit."

Amber played them on her mind like shadows on a wall, singing the visions to the impatient dragon, calling on her peace and sharing it. The compulsion to jump soon calmed. The dragon returned to its cave deep in Amber's chest, burrowed into her heart to sleep and watch through its dreams. Amber didn't understand it, how a creature could live through its dreams. She'd only heard it whisper of this state. Amber released the elder's hand.

"The dragon is calm now," Amber said, exhausted. "I don't know if I can do this."

"You regret accepting the spirit?"

"I had heard of the dragon carriers, the spirit warriors. But I didn't understand."

"They awoke to fight the darkness we humans created with our soulless machines, but they don't possess a physical form. Old elemental spirits of place. A deep dragon dwelled in this mountain, one of the oldest of its kind."

Amber sipped her tea. It had cooled but still retained its flavor. The tea tasted sweeter, kinder, and she gulped. The infusion soothed her stomach and calmed her spirit. The elder must have known the struggle Amber had suffered; of course, this is why she'd come to the mountain to seek the elder's help.

"Where did the dragons come from?"

"They embody the elemental forces of this world. Rivers run with their spirit. Deserts burn with their souls. Each natural place has a spirit. The natural forces spontaneously created them, and the dragons slept until needed."

"And now we need them."

"We have poisoned the world. And what we've created has also drawn life and spirit. This planet cannot help it. The dark ones live in the old cities, and we of flesh dwell in the green lands. Now rest, and we will talk more of your journey in the morning."

She finished the tea and curled up by the fire. The elder took out a fur from her pouch and covered her legs to help her keep warm. "One more question."

"Just the one, then you both shall dream."

"Will I ever grow wings?"

"Perhaps. None have ever. But there is a hope that the dream can be made flesh. Their kind has joined with ours for ten seasons now—so many children of the natural world. They are the raw spirit of nature—of the ocean, lakes, the mountains, the forests. You have a young one in you. Your spirit and the dragon's are imbalanced. It is too powerful, and your body is not designed to be its vessel.

110

Your spirit is carved by river beds and empty canals where your own soul energies flow, filling channels, pumping like blood through veins. Your companion tries to flow through these veins also, and so much of your fear fills you."

"I have dreamed of a dark dragon, made of ash and soot," Amber said, closing her eyes. "It haunts me when I sleep."

The elder emptied the teapot then through herbs on the fire. A sweet scent wafted over the hillside, calming Amber, helping her to sleep—and putting to calm the dragon spirit rooted into her heart.

"That is the shadow dragon. Your fear. It haunts you both."

"I was supposed to be watching my sister," Amber said. "My fear hunts me."

"Nothing hunts you, it is not real," the elder said.

"How can I fight it?" asked Amber.

"You cannot," advised the elder. "It is not real. Now sleep. Dream."

*Trust me.*

In the dream, she felt the voice of the dragon spirit. Letters wrote in the sky, formed of nebulous cloud matter and wind, blown and woven through, carved into the fabric of the night sky—or perhaps it was written onto her eyes. She saw more than the words. Amber sensed the emotions behind each phrase. Words were just symbols. In waking, the dragon's language, its means of communication overwhelmed her brain, but the spirit dreamed. It could read, perceive, feel deeper than the body, and in dreams, the spirit was emancipated from flesh.

*I feel your fear.*

"I failed her," Amber said, speaking to the sky. She flew over the countryside, gliding over a forest. She descended fast, losing altitude, heading for a patch of evergreens. She didn't know how to fly. "I'm going to hit!"

*Focus. You have wings.*

"I'm a human. All we do is fall."

*You doubt yourself.*

"I am too weak. I can't save her."

*Try to fly.*

"I can't!" The ground raced for her, and she wobbled, clawing at the air, trying to find something onto which to hold. Death came fast. The wind blew her auburn curls. A shadow flew over the treetops, soaring near.

*We share wings. Feel them.*

She focused, listening to his words. The dragon spirit sent her visions of birds and butterflies flapping wings. Amber felt their spirit, found their essence and let them fuse into her spirit. Wings sprouted from her shoulders. Muscles grew from her arms, spreading out. Bone emerged. Feathers sprung from her new limbs, and she practiced flapping the wings by flexing her upper body. Flying required use of every muscle in her body, and Amber concentrated, using the discipline taught by her grandmother. She focused and learned the rhythm of flight. Eventually, she lifted, rising above the ground, accelerating as she worked her new appendages.

*There now. We are free.*

Her heart beat like hummingbird wings, and Amber's blood warmed, passing through her system like hot stew. She flew higher, rising into the clouds. But she sensed it—a coming heaviness weighing her down. Darkness spread like spilled ink into the sky.

*Prepare yourself.*

The dragon terror speared through the cloudbank. Mist swirled around it in an eddy then dropped like a tide, flowing down over the land below. The beast was the size of a hill. Six wings dominated the horizon. Eyes covered its

113

serpentine head and neck. It roared, and clawed tendrils lashed at the air.

"We cannot fight this."

*Then what will you do?*

The creature bore down on them. Amber could fly away or try to fight it, but she didn't believe she could defeat the beast. It would consume them either way. Wouldn't it be better to die in a fight, to stand as a warrior? "How can I fight this fear?"

*Can you fight fear—or run from it?*

Amber pushed harder against the air, flying faster, diving for the heart of the creature. She didn't seek her bow nor did she bite at its flesh. Either would be futile. She calmed herself with her warrior's focus and closed her eyes, waiting to drown in the fear. When she opened them, the fear creature had evaporated, dissipated into dark mist then nothingness.

"What became of it?"

*It was never real. And now you are real.*

Amber awoke a new being. Her spirit had lightened, and she jumped to her fight, ready to fight. The shadow in the city, the old technology truly couldn't hurt her. The elder had slept with her, lying head to head, and she stood with her teacher.

"How do you know so much?"

The elder's eyes flared, shining red. The silhouette of a dragon flowed from her body and painted along the flesh and bone. She possessed the mountain dragon, an old one. Amber could sense the ancient spirit, and they had come here to teach. "We hoped a true spirit would come. You are the first who has bonded with her spirit. You will become our redemption."

Amber stood on the edge of the cliff and watched the hawks. She focused, concentrating, letting the fear slip from her. You couldn't fight an illusion and only fueled it with your struggle. You had to release it and not engage it in battle. "You must pick your battles," she said, lifted her arms above her head then leaped off the cliff. She trusted her younger brother to lift her and recalled how to fly. Spirit wings spun of energy emerged from her back. Feathers of light sprouted from the structure, and she flexed her shoulders, flapping her wings. She flew from the hill and soared over the countryside. Amber covered the distance and appeared over her clan's camp. Her brothers and sisters looked up at her and cheered, taking hope in the

115

sight of her flight. Then she turned, aiming for the old city, flying right into the dark heart of the techno-demon. From above, the city looked like a broken toy, a forgotten plaything left to decay and rot, passed off by children. Humans didn't need the old ways. Metal flowed at the heart, thickening and concentrating, feeding out from the middle like veins down limbs. Black crawlers strolled along the steel constructs—spiders weaving webs on the shattered buildings and roads.

The dark spirit pulsed at the heart of the city. Ebony waves flowed from the giant sphere. Cords whipped and spun, tapping naked humans, almost loving them like a mother. The human slaves worked, feeding furnaces, carrying recovered metal and plastic, building the empire of the techno-demons. The dark heart beheld Amber on her attack run. Crimson eyes pierced the charcoal dust clouds and tentacles soon followed, lashing for her, ripping at the warrior.

Visions of a river flowing into an ocean filled Amber's inner mind. She understood and let the energy flow through her, releasing the young dragon, allowing it to become her. She held her spirit, keeping the dragon in check, knowing her own strength. The darkness clawed her, hitting her body, and she hit back. Talons emerged from her hands. The green dragon's body glowed like light shining through an emerald, and a verdant aura radiated from her body. She opened her mouth to sing the songs of her grandmother, and a yellow light poured from her lips, drilling into the metal heart of the demon. Its spirit faded, overwhelmed by their light. The old city died. The souls of the dead who had lived through the centuries finally slept.

Amber flew above the mass of slaves that she had freed. Their minds slowly returned to them now that the demons had died and silenced. Amber's grandmother cried when the warrior carried Lanna into their tent. Then she returned to the world, flying to the next city and the next, emancipating her kind and teaching new dragon warriors, showing them her dreams. And they'd never forget the old world as the dragons and the humans made a new one.

# Tipping the Scales
*Dorian Graves*

It was an ill omen when the morning "Counting of Assets and Devouring of Sheep" ritual was interrupted. The fact that this was done by polite knocking, not barging in with weapons swinging, somehow made it worse.

My boss was in human form at the time, meaning he was civil enough to use silverware on his mutton. Sparks still flew on his breath when he shouted, "Ms. Cleese! Were you foolish enough to schedule a ten AM without telling me?"

"Of course not, sir. I'll go see who it is." I set down the emerald I was examining, adjusted my glasses, and checked the peephole. Two figures; a man with ragged hair and ruddy skin, the other a woman who was sharp-dressed about a century too late. Both were swaddled by thick robes, which obscured their faces. They sniffed the air as if they could smell me through the door. "Vampires, sir."

"I know that. They reek." My boss tapped his nose, which he claimed could sense any supernatural entity and valuable treasure. "I mean, which of the imbeciles are outside the door? In broad daylight, no less."

118

"They are properly dressed for it, sir. I do believe it's the new leader of the Broodmothers, and our contact from Dracula's Dogs. Shall I let them in?"

Boss humphed as he stood up. "I will. Ms. Cleese, prepare the room."

That simple order meant to simultaneously hide the assets, close the blackout curtains, and make sure the most uncomfortable chairs were out for those who showed up without appointment. I hurried at a speed still achingly slow to the non-humans behind me. The boss answered our visitors with sharp manners; I didn't need to look to bet that his claws were unsheathed and scraping the doorknob.

"Do sit. Either of you interested in tea? Mutton?" Boss smirked with his teeth, knowing full well that his guests couldn't indulge in either. I wouldn't say he was vindictive, but a jerk? Most definitely. "I do know why you're here, by the way. So, who goes first?"

"Pardon?" The Broodmother leader asked while her rival demanded "Whaddya' mean by that?" Both winced upon sitting. The Dracula Dog's eyes flickered to me, standing by the curtains. He snarled. I nodded and pretended to open the curtains. He flinched, then snarled again.

Boss ignored this. "You're here to barter for my services in front of each other, instead of in-secret. We're at the point where this petty feud is more a matter of pride than anything. My favorite part, I must admit." His claws drummed on the table. "I do clean up the reckless so well."

The Broodmother pulled back her hood to show her sculpted face, with matching cold eyes. "We are not so foolish. Has no one informed you of last night?"

Boss leaned forward. The Dracula Dog leaned back. Both recognized that the woman's tone was not one to be directed at a dragon. She did not, marking her naivety. Boss clicked his tongue. "Ms. Cleese? Inform our guests about last night. And do pour them some tea; they look dry as a priest."

"As you wish." I stood between the vampires, noting how their lips curled away from their fangs at the sight of the drink. "Last night was rather busy. We took out a hunter for the local wolves, and fought not one but three self-proclaimed Chosen Ones. Two fledgling wizards and a madman respectively. We took the last one home to burn in the fireplace for our evening Scrabble match." Which Boss cheated at, putting together random letters and claiming they were in "dragon-tongue." Of course, one never tells a

120

dragon to play by the rules.

The vampires gazed into their tea, up at my neck, back at their tea. They did look paler than normal, skin more like parchment than flesh. I didn't see any wounds on them, but vampires tend to heal those quickly. The Dracula Dog spoke, "The clans were attacked last night. Chased like dogs, burnt to crisps. Some of the clans, like the Ninth Street Fangs, were wiped off the map."

"Sounds like my kind of party." Boss beckoned me over before our guests could give in and eat me instead of ignoring their tea. "Who will I enact your vengeance on, then? Did the angels get too uppity? Or wait—let me guess, one of your own interrupted a mage's ritual, and now your own blood burns in your veins. Maybe even both!" The drumming of claws turned into scraping the well-worn grooves of the desk, down to the drawer where gold-encrusted pens waited to bleed ink on contracts. "In which case, let me remind you of my typical fees."

"Let us finish first!" The Broodmother barked, face crinkling to break the sculpted façade. The Dracula Dog scooted his seat back as she continued, "Neither are the case. Whatever it was, we never sensed it coming. It didn't even register as human, but as…nothing. But it had claws,

121

it breathed fire, and we could not pierce its hide. Nor its wings."

It was rare that I saw Boss caught off-guard. That moment when his irises went red, his composure shaken just enough for gilded scales to litter his skin. The Broodmother's words fit together in his head, and the idea they formed were not approved of.

In his stead, I asked the Dracula Dog, "Can you attest to this?"

"Yeah ma'am. I barely saw it, too busy running, but…it looked like a dragon, felt like jack."

Claws raked new paths in the desk. "Then it is not a dragon. If one were in the city, I would know. The whole city would." And that time when Boss smiled, it was the vicious grin of a psychopath—which in all honesty fit my boss to a T. "An imposter, on the other hand…that's something I'll need to look into. Ms. Cleese? Interview our friend here in the hallway."

Boss pointed at the Dracula Dog. I grabbed a notebook. "Very well, sir. What about our other friend?"

"I will take care of her personally. It's the least I can do."

The Dracula Dog scurried behind me as we strode out

the door. "This isn't part of the interview," I told him, "but do you think Boss will open the windows first, or just set her on fire?"

"Even if I were a betting man," the vampire hissed from under his hood, "I wouldn't take that guess. Too morbid."

Laughter drifted from the other side of the door. Hot on its heels were screaming, and then the sliding of curtains. "Fire breath first. He does love to add insult to injury. Now, if you'll be so kind as to follow me…"


"…and you even have this so-called social justice for your sheep. Who in their right mind gives agency to their food?"

As we stalked the streets, Boss informed me about the many things wrong with humans, one of his favorite topics of conversation. The morning was bright but brisk, so the streets were empty of most who would run from my boss, who appeared an almost-seven-foot man with the crimson suit and two-tone hair, also known. In fact, the streets only held old and oblivious humans, who Boss didn't chase as a rule because they were "so easy, it's a crime."

Boss stopped at a street sign, closing his eyes to sense out the nearby supernaturals. "Ms. Cleese, where do you think we should start? The wizards have taken up most of

Main Street, but the Atlantians in the park are far more interesting to speak with. Then again, my coat might get wet..."

"May I instead suggest heading downtown?" I pulled out the morning newspaper, headlines screaming about suspected arson in that very area, with more mundane articles about upcoming elections and a recent string of car thefts. "Our antagonist was said to breathe fire, after all, and that is the area where most of the vampire clans were..."

Boss snatched the paper, eyes darting across the page before handing it back. "Excellent choice, Ms. Cleese. Your lesser thoughts do wonders at times."

I took the paper back with no complaint. Were I to have an official job description, duties would include performing mundane tasks and thinking the aforementioned lesser thoughts, which meant all things my boss believed beneath him. This used to offend me as a child, but I soon realized that his arrogance eclipsed the existence of all others. At least I was a small blip in his personal radar.

The newspaper photos did not hold a candle to reality. Small stores that were once vampire bases were little more than cinder, remnants of metal beams and cracked concrete poking out of the smoldering wreckage. Apartment windows were black from smoke. We passed by the wreckage of a classic Mercedes that looked like a pack of elephants had used it for a mosh pit; the snarling face of the Dracula Dog's logo on the hood was almost bent beyond recognition. I thought myself jaded to carnage, but this was on a mass level even my boss refrained from. I zipped up my jacket to cover my face.

Boss stepped into the rubble, taking a deep breath of the smoke. He stuck his tongue out as if tasting something foul. "Gah! Definitely not dragon fire. It tastes like gasoline." He tilted his head up and smacked his lips. "No, diesel. Even worse."

"But something big was definitely through here," I said, pointing to the car and the fresh craters in the street. "No humans, or tools around here, could do that. Even the strongest werewolf would be hard-pressed…right?"

"Unless fueled by steroids and a temper tantrum, and even then…" Boss strode to one of the craters. It was about the size of a two-person restaurant table, with thick grooves on the outside clawing inward. Much like the claws on Boss' desk, in fact. He stepped in it, one foot in the middle, and traced calculations through the air. Shook his head

125

before kneeling, putting his palm against the center instead. A low growl rumbled through the air when he stood back up.

"It shouldn't be able to hide so easily, if it's as large as…" Boss shook his head before returning to me. "Cleese! Search the area. I am off to find witnesses." He stomped a few feet away before looking up at the apartments. "We've had business here before, yes?"

"With many vampires, sir." Which he knew full well, but I caught the meaning of his question. He needed a distraction from his theories. "And there was that mortal with a sacred blade, the one who seduced the angel and demon rivals. Remember?"

Boss' lips curled into a smile that was all teeth. "Ah, yes. And when they raised a ruckus, I kidnapped both lovers and had the mortal choose who to free. Except I burned both!" A wicked chuckle snaked through his throat. "Perhaps she's seen something. I may as well ask her. Fourth floor, apartment seventeen, yes?"

"Yes. She did try to kill you last year, boss."

"Of course. Think she'll try again? I could use a nice duel around now. I might even play fair and stick to fisticuffs." He waggled his fingers at me in a sort of wave as he departed for the hotel. I couldn't recall if, by his definition, fisticuffs included claws or not. Doubtless I would find out after investigating. I watched to make sure he entered the building without incident, then began my search in earnest.

I began to take notes, estimating the force necessary to break the streets themselves or the heat required to melt through metal, when my cellphone rang. It was a text from one of my few relatives in the city, Willis. He was confirming the time for a luncheon we had planned; I texted back, in between notes, that I would have to cancel.

"It's about those fires, isn't it?" Came his reply. "Something to do with your work?"

Willis was one of the few in my family who knew about my eccentric career, and believed me instead of writing me off as mad. I texted back, "Something is attacking the local supernaturals. Supposedly a robot. Took out most of the vampires already." I also asked him a quick question about melting vehicles; he was still in college, an engineering major. I stopped next to a convenience store as I waited for his reply. I tried to ask the store's owner if she'd seen anything, but she only spoke Spanish, which was one of Boss' many tongues but not mine.

As I tried to write her words down anyway, Willis responded with a complex formula, followed by, "With something that hot, no wonder the vampires got smoked out. Ha ha? Anyway, any places I should avoid if this bot's on the loose?"

This was around the time the clashing started. The old woman and I both stared up at the apartments, where the silent smoking was interrupted by banging and crashing. It sounded like Boss got the fight he wanted. Except that a figure with red hair and a shining white blade hit the fire escape and kept running—that was the woman Boss went to interview, but the noises didn't stop with her departure. In fact, they seemed to get louder, as if trying to drown out the clack of her high-heels on the metal stairs.

I tugged the store owner's sleeve. "Ma'am, I suggest we move. Quickly." She must have understood at least the urgency in my voice, because she followed me as we left the storefront. Moments later, my boss was tossed out an apartment window and sailed through the air. Before he had a chance to hit anything, wings burst through his coat like a pair of golden kites. He spat fire into the debris below before charging back in. I caught a glimpse beforehand of the metal head watching from the window, almost mistakable for a vehicular crane bursting from the building, chrome glinting like scales in the artificial red light given off by the glowing eyes. Digging into the edge of the windowsill, even after Boss crashed into it again, were blades twisted into the shape of claws, lacking the scrapes and breaks from millennia of fighting.

The old woman screamed. Most mortals couldn't see magical beings like my boss in their true form, not for long. Their brains fractured with tiny cracks first to tell them it was an illusion, a staged act, a dream. But the monster in the window, currently trying to take a hefty bite out of my boss' shoulder, was a beast of metal instead of magic. A punch from Boss didn't even dent its frame, just made the light of one eye flicker like old neon signs.

"Get out of here, alright?" I told the woman, motioning down the street to make my point. "Get somewhere safe." She shook her head, and remained frozen to the spot until I heard a crash behind us. The woman fled as I heard a snort, but the draconic android was gone from the window—it must have left while I was distracted. Did it think my boss dead, or not worth its time? I considered following, but my first priority was my boss. I turned to the cement-and-glass rubble, where the corner store had broken Boss' fall. He pulled himself out with dust in his two-tone hair; golden scales had replaced his skin, a reflex to mitigate the damage of the fall.

"Cleese? Ms. Cleese, was this building on our list of acceptable collateral damage?"

I took off my glasses to wipe the dust from them. "When you visited this store to kidnap that one demon, you did complain about the quality of the slushies, sir."

"Excellent." Boss stood up and brushed the debris off his sleeves. "It seems someone has made a robotic mockery of yours truly, Ms. Cleese. You saw it, correct?"

"I saw it leave after throwing you out a window. Twice, I may add."

Boss flashed a smile full of fangs. "Indeed, I didn't expect it to have the strength of an actual dragon. A lesser one, of course."

"Of course." I put my glasses back on and examined the apartment once more. The android was gone. So was the old woman, the mortal Boss had gone to interview, any signs of life.

"What do you think it's here for? Mindless destruction, or do you think it's programmed for more?"

"Does it matter?" Boss rolled his shoulders and stepped

out of the rubble. The scales fled from his skin, but the sharp teeth remained. "I've lived too long to bother with excuses. We're going to crush that mockery, then we crush whoever made it. Simple, isn't it?"

"As simple as it is elegant, sir." It wouldn't do to argue and end up on the crush list, after all.

As we left, I remembered to text Willis back. I gave him a quick list of supernatural hotspots to avoid—such as the wizard's council on Main Street, the Celestial and Infernal Embassies on opposite ends of town, and the woods where the werewolves frequented—and a warning to stay safe. He texted back, "You too. See if you can stay inside and out of this whole mess?"

I could have told him I'd try, but danger was a lifestyle hazard when dragons were involved. So instead, I texted a lie and continued to follow my boss as he explained his newest scheme. I quietly jotted down notes on 'suggestions' to improve upon it later. All part of the job, I told myself.

I thought Boss was a robot too, when I first met him after he kidnapped my parents. I was not the only child this happened to; in fact, I was the tenth one that day. My cousins were taken to this warehouse before me, told that their loved ones were on the other side, and then shoved in. No one told them about the dragon, and my cousins said nothing about it afterwards. They were shaken, shivering and crying—but when asked what they'd seen, they couldn't answer. Their parents were released soon afterwards to comfort each child.

Willis had been there too. He had actually managed to comprehend what was inside for a few minutes, before his mind snapped. He had curled up in a corner and cried about how his mother was going to be eaten whole. I had never seen him so pale.

I did not know that this was a task set up by my great-aunt, to see who she would train to be the dragon's next assistant. All I knew was that the warehouse was smoky, and there was a giant, winged lizard in the middle of it. But it wasn't moving, just watching me with what I'd learn was a trademark smirk. It didn't have room to chase anyone like the dinosaurs had in Jurassic Park. Plus, it was yellow. There was nothing scary about the color yellow.

So I walked across the room. When the dragon put a claw in the way, I climbed over the scaled fingers, each one thicker than both my hands put together, and kept going. I only paused when the dragon arced its head over mine and flicked fire from its tongue.

"That's not real fire," I said, more to convince myself than anything else.

"Would you like me to test it on your mother, then?" The dragon sounded like it was laughing.

"Nuh-uh. She burns herself cooking all the time anyway."

The dragon narrowed its green eyes, until they were slits like a cat's. "Do you even know what I am?"

"An animaton...animanatronic...a robot dragon. Like at the park with the roller-coasters."

The creature I assumed was a robot raised an eyebrow. Smoke dribbled from its breath. "A dragon, you say? You know those aren't real."

"Daddy said the same about the monster under the bed, but he still got me a flashlight. And now there's no monster, 'cause I hit it in the face. But that broke the flashlight, so I need a new one." I looked to my father, to see if he got the hint, but he only watched in wide-eyed terror. I looked back to the dragon.

Except that there wasn't a dragon anymore, but a tall man with a red suit and blond hair—he hadn't yet dyed the top layer black—walking out of the warehouse. My parents ran to me and cried, and I thought it was because they were worried for me, or maybe themselves. I didn't realize then that actually seeing the dragon was equivalent to passing an interview. Training, everything from secretary work to swordplay, would soon follow.

When we left the warehouse, my great-aunt said I was going to live with her and her master for a bit. She told me the man's name, a grumbling, snarling thing I still can't pronounce. I tried, even as my parents begged her not to take me. Willis watched from the corner with watery eyes.

They all stopped when the man in the crimson coat came back. I didn't, until the man crouched in front of me. "You. What is your name? Your full name, I mean."

"Polly!" My great-aunt frowned with all of her wrinkles. "I mean, Pauline Angelina Cleese."

I almost began to recite the spelling, like at school. But the strange man interrupted, ruffling my hair and saying, "That's a big name. Like mine. So I shall call you Ms. Cleese, and you can call me Boss. Sounds brilliant, doesn't it?"

I would later come to realize that it sounded as arrogant and as blatantly informal as the rest of him. But in the end, both then and now, I decided I didn't really mind.

"The only reason it caught me off-guard was that it literally appeared from nothing. Some sort of…invisibility trick." Boss huffed as he scribbled a diagram of the robot from memory. "No self-respecting dragon would ever turn invisible. We have no need to. Whoever made this scrapheap has no true idea what they're dealing with."

We were back in the office, trying to come up with a course of action. Not only did we have to find the metal monstrosity, but we had to figure out where it came from. Diesel was a common enough smell in this city that tracking by scent, Boss' usual preference, would be useless. I had suggested a number of tracking devices, but that would still involve finding the robot and tagging it without alerting it that something was up.

I still added the trackers to my list of supplies to drag from Boss' hoard. Hidden amongst the treasures were a number of devices he had no use for, but that I could use to my advantage. Handling the technology for him was another unsung skill in my possession.

"Here. This is what I recall beyond it trying to shove its crude claws in my face." Boss handed me his diagram. He was no artist, but the front of the robot matched what I'd seen. Plus, there were circles and arrows around various parts. Boss tapped once such arrow and explained, "Anatomical errors. Whoever made this has never seen a real dragon."

"Or doesn't possess your flawless memory of anatomy." Judging from the boss' notes, the robot was squatter and boxier than a true dragon, its tail too short for proper balance and its nose so close to the mouth that breathing in sparks from the flames was almost guaranteed. Other notes included "absolutely hideous" and "teeth too dull for proper devouring of sheep." I could have pointed out that robots needed neither food nor to attract mates, but I also could've asked Boss to set my hair on fire to see what would happen.

A low growl rumbled outside. Boss scowled, but then sniffed the air and let the expression pass for something far more devious. "I do believe I have a plan. Ms. Cleese, to the door! We have pawns—I mean, dear guests—who are waiting."

I went to see which poor saps would be roped into the dragon's schemes this time. The one growling was a werewolf we'd actually assisted the night before, one Vanessa Howlsing. Her ire was directed at an angel I hadn't met before. Both were attempting to maintain a human form, but the angel glowed with feathers poking from under clothing, while the werewolf had fixed her fur but forgot to remove the under-bite or snout. I invited them in before they could be noticed and offered them tea.

"Yer a good one, Cleesey," Howlsing accepted as she pulled a shimmering necklace out of her oversized trenchcoat. "I brought the payment, includin' this shiner."

"Surely, such trivial pursuits can wait," the angel intoned. "An abomination stalks the streets; its removal must come before any other arrangements."

"Ain't you a pup? First rule of dealing wit dragons, never put off the payday." She strode into the office with a pride not many others in the city could manage. "Boss! You're lookin'…well, pissed, if I wanna' be honest."

Boss stopped digging his pen through the diagram. "From you, Howlsing, I'll allow it. Go on, sit down." He pointed the pen at the angel, as if ready to shred through those feathers next. "And you are?"

"Jesandriel, Bearer of the Sacred Arrows and—"

The pen pointed to the other free chair. "Jesse it is, then. Take your seat."

The angel frowned. "I just told you, my name is—"

137

"Jesse, I get it. Or I can just call you Feathertits like the rest of your kind. Sit down." Boss and Jesse glared at each other until the angel finally took their seat. Boss waited until I had brought the proffered tea before saying, "I suppose you're wondering why I called you here today."

Howlsing snorted into her cup. "You didn't call us. I just came t'pay, and Feathers came to be insulted, I guess." Jesse grumbled but looked just as confused. I suppose neither of them were much for movies.

"I may as well have called you here, because I have use for the both of you. Truly, your timing is impeccable." Boss revealed his diagram, which now bore more than a few holes. "Someone has made a machine mockery of myself—the nerve, I know—and is using it to attack my prey. Most of the vampires have already been eliminated, which means my evenings are going to be significantly less entertaining."

"This is why I came to speak with you," Jesse stated. They still hadn't touched the tea. "This beast's reign of terror has spread to both the Celestial and Infernal Embassies. Many of us had to be recalled for repairs." Despite keeping statue-still, the disdain was clear in the angel's voice. "We few remaining have not been cleared to

138

use any sacred relics; such could disrupt the human populace. Thus we were hoping, out of the kindness of your heart…"

I coughed. Howlsing sniggered into her tea again. Boss smirked as he mocked the angel's pose, hands folded in his lap. "Kindness? None of that, I'm afraid, but I have plenty of rage to go around. I'll be happy to fight the fake and whoever made it…and that's where you two come in."

Were Howlsing in wolf-form, her ears surely would've folded back. "Hey, I just came over to pay you off. Ya' don't need to rope me in."

"Consider this a change in the terms of payment. Your help would make us equal, for now, and you can save those pretty baubles for later transactions." Which, if the werewolves didn't find trouble themselves, Boss was sure to make some; I saw the way he'd eyed the necklace Howlsing had shown off. "Your task is simple. See where this robotic foe goes. Take note if it tracks down particular targets, like the rest of the vampires. Or if it stops anywhere to refuel—it runs on diesel, reeks of the stuff. Any important information, call me immediately." He smiled and raised a finger, allowing the nail to warp into a claw. "But no matter what happens, don't reveal yourselves by interfering. Just call me."

There was elegance to hiring those two. While the robot could turn invisible, Howlsing's superior (though Boss was loathe to admit it) sense of smell would allow her to continue tracking without sight. As for the angel, it would continue the chase to the end of time if it had to, out of sheer tenacity. At least one of them would capture the android eventually—and if not, at least Boss would have fun watching them run in circles.

Perhaps suspecting the latter, Jesse scoffed. A pair of cloud-white wings flapped behind them in annoyance. "I follow the orders of God, and none other."

"If your God doesn't like it, then He can come down and fight me. It's been far too long since I fought a deity." Boss flashed his teeth, smoke seeping from the cracks. A brief moment turned his pupils into cold-blooded slits.

Before the boss had a chance to show off any more, the angel shut up and agreed to listen. Smartest choice they made that day; it takes weeks to air dragon smoke out of a building.

Do not think that Boss did nothing while we awaited our call to action. He trusted others to his dirty work, but he was far more impatient than expected of a man a few millennia old. So he called out more eyes to watch the city, and for once made said calls himself. He told me this was because I lacked the strength of conviction. Translation: I was just a human and had a hard time intimidating monsters into working without promise of pay.

I made my own preparations. While not much of a fighter, I had my own armor to protect against collateral damage—a gift from my now-distant parents, though the ornate gloves were a holiday gift from Willis. I texted him to update him on the situation, but didn't get a response back. While waiting, I ordered a few military-grade EMPs, which would arrive in a few days. And, in case of absolute emergency, I grabbed the Dragontongue. As the name suggests, it is a sharp red sword that resembles the tongue my boss sticks out at me when feeling particularly childish. I doubted it would do much against metal, but it was better than nothing.

I asked Boss as I checked my gear, "Why do you think the android was built? Just the destruction of the local supernaturals?"

"I'd like to think I do a good enough job of that." Boss nudged a nearby phone; he was waiting for the local wizard's parliament to reach a decision. They had only agreed to try agreeing on something once their research was put under threat of dragon fire; their base on Main Street had been attacked an hour ago. "In the grand scheme of life, reasons don't amount to much, so why bother? This abomination has attacked my city and mocked my glory by existing. So it goes, and so does anyone who thought it was a good idea."

"As expected. But out of curiosity sir, I must ask…" I waited for Boss to give me the okay to go ahead. He considered before waving at me to continue. "Sir, if someone were to pay you for what we assume is the same job, to take out all that is supernatural in the city…would you?"

He snorted, flames licking the corners of his nostrils. "It wouldn't be the first time someone's offered. The cost is always far greater than they can hope to pay." He gestured out the window, open and streaming sunlight. The trash can nearby still held the Broodmother's ashes. "For you see, this is more than just a city to me, just as its citizens are more than just people. Do you know what I mean?"

I grabbed the Dragontongue's golden hilt, and let the crimson blade shimmer in the light. "I would be a poor assistant if I didn't. This city is one you built out of sand. Its citizens are the toys you haven't thrown out. And the robot? An unexpected, low-quality 'surprise' someone left in your metaphorical sandbox."

"And here I worried you'd think I liked the damn fools or something." Boss seemed to miss the fact that he'd just been compared to a toddler, which was all the better for my continued health. The phone rang before he could say more, and he answered expecting it was the wizards finally calling back. Then he started smiling. "Really, Howlsing? Do go on."

By the time Boss hung up and informed me that the android had been found, I had already closed up the office and finished arming myself. The EMPs were still a few days off, so I'd have to manage the fight without the help of technology. Regrettable, but not impossible.

"Remember the old high school that had the cult in its basement? That's where we're going."

"Excellent. Shall I start the motorcycle up, Boss?"

He shook his head, and strode past me to the door. "An impression needs to be made. The only suitable way to travel shall be as myself."

"But the humans—"

"Will mistake me for one of their school-buses. Or a low-flying plane. Either way, an acceptable blow to my pride for the cause." My boss' claws were already unsheathed, horns breaking through his forehead. For a second, he looked more devil than dragon. I certainly cannot argue against him being both.

My fellow humans have a bad habit of fantasizing what it's like to ride on a dragon. I will correct all misconceptions now: It's horrible. They hate anyone near the base of their wings, and both the neck and tail are lanky things unsuitable to sit on. Plus, there are the ridges to consider. So while the trip only took fifteen minutes, I spent the time almost hanging off a dragon's backside, practically doing the splits as I sat, thankful for the gloves that kept the sharp ridges from cutting my hands.

I made a mental note that the next time the Boss decided it was his birthday—an arbitrary date whose true time was lost long ago—it was worth the temper tantrum to get him a saddle.

The old school still wore burn marks and police tape. A reluctant pang hit my chest. I had infiltrated this school when I was younger in order to find the wayward cult in its depths. Willis had even joined in, always made a game about us being a duo of spies. Even with him along and Boss lurking over my shoulder, it was one of the few times I'd been primarily surrounded by humans and had normal friends. I'd envied them at the time. Seeing how the sight of the ruins affected me, perhaps I still did.

Boss clawed through a hole in the building's side, announcing his presence with an ear-wrenching shriek. Howlsing echoed from her hiding place, and the angel hid all distaste for my boss when they followed him inside. I grasped the hilt of Dragontongue and followed; any envy I may have had didn't stand a chance to the mounting adrenaline.

Even if robots hadn't invaded the hallways when we did, I still wouldn't call the building empty. Debris covered the floor, dust caked into the carpets. Broken lockers vomited left-behind textbooks and backpacks. One had a fishbowl with a tiny ball of rot floating in the musty water. Parts of the wall were caved in, obscuring signs for the upcoming school dance. One such poster had been painted by my hand. A robot, this one more humanoid than draconic, crashed into it seconds after I saw it.

The androids looked like B-movie creations. The glow

145

of green eyes glinted off their boxy metal frames—their noses and mouths were little more than slits. Most of their weaponry were just guns and swords welded to their arms. Intimidating, but not more so than the werewolf ripping off said arms, or the angel firing arrows into their flat faces. Boss didn't bother with those small fry; any he destroyed were on accident as he barreled through hallways he was almost didn't fit through.

I tried to follow, but three robots blocked my path I unsheathed Dragontongue and swung the blade into my attackers. The blade, red-hot like the beasts it was modeled after, melted through the metal. Core wires and circuits now burnt up, the robots fell into the debris, limbs flailing as they short-circuited. I continued the swings regardless, striking any contraption that came into range as I carved a path after my employer.

"Human, your martial skills are most uncanny," Jesse called behind me. We were back to back for a minute of the fight, the wind from their wing beats unnaturally warm. Most humans are surprised to learn that angels are actually warmer than demons; comes from a lifetime living in the light. "Lady Cleese, are you sure you are solely human?"

"Y'saying a human can't kick some cans around,

Feathers?" Howlsing mocked, barely intelligible through a mouthful of wires. "That's species-ist or somethin'. Boss just hires the best a' the best, is all."

"The things I put up with for Him," the angel grumbled through their expressionless face. An arrow swooshed past my ears and struck a robot ahead of me. "Human or not, I do not see why you put up with that dragon. If you ever wish for another avenue of employment…"

I shook my head and let Flametongue weave through the last wave of robots before me. There were more than I expected; whoever made these had far too much time on-hand. "I may just be mortal—Boss made sure of that—but I wouldn't give this job up for the world. Now, there's a certain someone I need to regroup with; cover for me?"

I believe Jesse was disappointed by my response, but Howlsing just barreled through the robots remaining in my path with a sound more hyena than wolf. "Said like a true pack-mate! You'd make a good wolf, kid, but no pushin' here. Go catch up with Boss; we've got things here."

I thanked them, gave Flametongue a last swing, and hurried down the hallway. I passed an old classroom with a missing door, the desks long broken and seats overturned. I shoved back the tide of memories until a later time, a time after the fight.

I caught up with Boss as he rounded a corner, only to see him be struck back into a wall. He snarled. A loose light fixture fell on his head. The air before him rippled, revealing the automatic draconic with one claw raised to strike him again. Boss head-butted the attacker in the chest with those spear-like horns of his, and then the two locked claws. It was like watching a wrestling match until they started shouting fire at each other.

I wish I could say that I charged into the fray, dodging blows that would've squished me to strike a key joint and lay the beast low. Maybe with a few flips and flourishes. Imagine I did that before I tell the truth. I hung back to watch the fight, debating if I should run and find the robot's creator or if it'd be better to stay in the rare case that Boss needed my help. But as I watched the fight, I caught sight of something under the android's tail: an exhaust pipe. I squinted, having left my glasses behind for this fight. Now that I looked, the robot's body was angled in familiar ways. Its back sloped at a slant to its neck, and just over the shoulders, I swore I saw door handles.

"Boss! Strike where its clavicle would be—it's built from a car!"

I might've had to state the obvious for Boss more often than not, but I never had to tell him something twice. The android tried to scurry away as Boss rent an uppercut claw just under the base of the neck. Sparks flew as he tore through the engine. The metal monster's visibility flickered as it crashed to the ground. The glowing eyes sputtered off.

Boss took a deep breath to finish it off. I raised a hand for him to stop, and not just because blowing up a car-based creature would blow me up too.

As I suspected, the metal dragon opened up—from the sunroof, to be precise. Out came a coughing man in an oil-stained lab coat. I knew Boss wanted to kill the man and be done with it, that he wouldn't recognize who this was, so I had to run over and grab the man as he escaped. He tried to pull away, but he was nowhere near as strong as his creation.

"Funny, how the embassies and the wizards were attacked after I told you not to go there." I tightened my grip on Willis' arm. Even without my glasses, there was no mistaking my cousin. "Going to explain what this is all about? Come up with something good, and I might convince Boss to let you go."

"I could say the same to you." Willis tried to glare at the

dragon, but could only manage a few seconds before terror replaced anger and he had to look away. "This guy's been corrupting you for years. Stole you from your family, and you don't even seem to care."

"So you tried to steal her away with a mockery?" Boss growled through a draconic throat not meant for human words. "What jealousy. Not that I'm surprised...I'm pretty admirable."

Willis shook his head, trembling even as he tried to pull away again. "I was trying to kill you! If there weren't any weird creatures in the city, then Polly could come back to us. And I figured, what could take out a dragon? Another dragon! A *better* one, because it's controlled by a human!"

Something about his excuse, his belief in his own malicious intentions, made me laugh. It was a laugh that sounded like my boss', sharp and mocking. I couldn't help the noise. The man watched in terror, slinking away as if I, too, was about to transform into a hideous beast.

"Listen to yourself! You just attacked a whole city, man and monsters alike. You've gotten people killed. And you think you're the hero here? That's so...human of you. It really is." I let him go, but I pointed Flametongue's tip at his chest. His eyes went to the gloves I held it with, the ones he'd bought me ages ago. "Maybe I have been corrupted. But what I do is important work. I maintain the balance of all the petty creatures in this city, human and monster alike. And Willis..."

I stepped forward. He stepped away, as if assuming I was about to gut him with my blade. I grabbed his hair instead and forced him to look at Boss in all his gilded glory. "I'm sorry Willis, but you just crossed the pettiest beast of them all. Who's also the most dangerous. Good job."

Like any human, his mind broke. I let go of his hair, and he fell to his knees a babbling mess. I could almost make out an apology in there, but we humans do have a skill of making something out of nothing. I turned and walked away over the mechanical corpse, knowing that Boss would give his enemy a gruesome end and deciding I didn't want to see it. I heard a scream and a crunch anyway. I kept walking until Boss fell into step with me, stumbling upon his readjustment to human form.

"Did you rip him up, or did you actually eat him?"

"Eat him? He smelled as bad as that trash he made, why would I eat that? I just squished him. He didn't even deserve to be burned."

"Of course." It crossed my mind that I had just let Boss kill one of the few family members I cared about. And I didn't feel guilty—I was more upset at Willis for having wrecked so much havoc on the city. "I think he's right, though. I have been…corrupted, you could say, by this line of work."

"Corrupted, or perhaps liberated? It all depends on how you look at things."

Boss focused on digging bits of metal out of his claws before turning them back to nails.

We passed by what used to be my locker. I saw the number hanging from the loose door; I'd never stored anything in it, but I still knew the combination. "You aren't surprised that I chose you over my own cousin—over a human like me?"

"You said it yourself; I'm the pettiest and strongest around. That's the job of a dragon. Curbing the pettiness and directing the power, that's what you do as my assistant. You play me the way I play everyone else in this city."

Boss let that sink in until we retraced our steps. The smaller robots had all fallen, and with their work done, Howlsing and Jesse had left. They hadn't said farewells, but I didn't feel bad—surely, we would run into both of them again soon enough. A city's a small place to a dragon and his kin, after all.

"Balance is the most important game," Boss finally said, "and it's the game we all play. You balance the mundane and all the important bits. That's your place, however you choose to accept it, Ms. Cleese."

"Good, because it almost sounded like you were insinuating that I'm just as power-hungry as every other creature in this city." Maybe he did, because Boss laughed after I said that anyway. "But if what you say is true, sir, then what do you balance?"

We reached the hole in the wall of the school ruins. The sky was blue and the sun was bright, and Boss looked up at the sky like he was ready to take his true form and try to eat the sun itself. Knowing him, I wouldn't be surprised if he'd tried at least once.

"Why, isn't it obvious? I'm the reminder that no matter how the odds are stacked against me, no one can tip these scales. Not man, not machine, and certainly no monster in this city." He could've clawed his way back out, but he decided to walk and offered his hand to me. "Now, hurry up Ms. Cleese. There's work to be done, meetings to ignore, and sheep to devour. Ready?"

I already knew that I was perhaps the only one in the city who'd be allowed to say no and walk away. It was a lot of work keeping up with a dragon, after all.

But in the end, both then and now, I realized I never really minded.

# How the Dragon Won a Battle in a Never-Ending War

*Denarose Fukushima*

Purple lightning cracked along the starry sky, outlining the gray clouds for a few seconds before fading to darkness. Large drops of rain plopped from slick blades of grass and splattered onto the ground.

A great clawed foot touched the soft earth as another bolt of lightning exploded above. Large, snake-like eyes slowly, meticulously scanned the riverbank, not a single drop of rain escaping their notice. A figure darker than a moonless night prowled out in the open, invisible to the untrained eye. The smell of fire and cherry blossom perfume was just barely discernable in the cold night air. Turning gracefully on his legs, the dragon followed the familiar scent.

He had almost reached the cave when Kiyohime sauntered out to greet him. The darkness did no justice to her sleek green scales; even her brilliant red underbelly looked dull. Indeed, daylight suited the colorful dragon much more.

"It's good of you to visit, Ryuga," she whispered. "I know how you detest leaving your lake."

"You weren't sleeping, were you?" her visitor asked, following her into the cave. Rows upon rows of ornate, glittering objects lined the cave walls; gilded mirrors, porcelain tea sets, ebony combs and intricately painted glassware all placed with care by Kiyohime, who loved pretty, impractical things.

"Why would I do something so silly after inviting you to my abode?" Kiyohime replied. But her voice sounded heavy, worn down. "I'm just surprised you came so late at night."

"You know as well as I do that it's the safest time to travel nowadays."

"Ah yes. Do you remember when dragons used to dance in the storms?" She blew a flame onto her makeshift fireplace and curled up next to it, staring sightlessly into the fire.

"It was so long ago...but yes, I remember it well." Ryuga sat across from her with the fire glowing between them.

"You've heard of the latest slayer?"

Ryuga looked up at the sound of Kiyohime's voice. It was an attempt at nonchalance, but not a very good one.

Kiyohime became excited very easily and the more dangerous the creature was, the more excited she got. One of her claws tapped the dirt eagerly, and Ryuga suppressed a sigh.

"I can't say that I have."

"Truly? He killed a horde of demons not too far off the coast," Kiyohime said. "He should be passing through in a few days, a week at most."

"Is that all you wanted to talk about?"

The smaller dragon cast her gaze downwards. "Ah, I forgot your dislike of small-talk. Forgive me. I invited you here to confirm a rumor I heard whispered among the shrubs not too long ago. A rumor about you."

Ryuga waited for her to go on. Though dragons were known for their solitary nature, Kiyohime seemed to struggle with the isolation. She tried not to be talkative when he came to visit, but still couldn't seem to sit comfortably in silence when there was someone she could be talking to or better yet, about. Ryuga tried to be patient.

"What rumors have you heard?"

"That there was an egg waiting for you in the west," she replied, large eyes fixed on him.

Ryuga closed his eyes and rested his head on his arms.

He wasn't surprised the word could spread so fast. But he was a little confused that Kiyohime would call him all the way to her home just to talk about it.

"The rumors are true," Ryuga said, still not opening his eyes.

Kiyohime was silent. The same three words kept running through Ryuga's mind.

*Please come back.*

Ryuga had received a letter containing news of the egg as well as a plea to be there for the hatchling. Ryuga would have preferred to raise the hatchling in his lands, but his mate had been insistent about him relocating.

"When will you leave, Ryuga?"

"Soon. I still have time."

"I would like it very much if you could stop here on your way out."

"I'll keep that in mind."

Kiyohime adjusted herself on the ground, eyes languidly going from Ryuga to the fire and back to Ryuga. She was probably wondering how much more she could get away with saying before he got irritated.

"Is it true that in the west, they name the child before it's born?"

"It is," Ryuga replied. It was a foreign practice, but he didn't mind it. "I'm sure his mother will have it all thought out by the time I arrive."

"His? How can you tell?"

"Call it a father's intuition."

"And you don't care to name him at all? I would want a say in his name, if I were you."

"Oh? And what would you name your young hatchling?" Ryuga asked.

Kiyohime stood and maneuvered around her cave, idly picking up a bell and inspecting it closely. She clicked on the side with her claw.

"Well, I would want to wait until after he was born to name him, that's for sure. However, I suppose if I couldn't think of anything else, and if his father wouldn't mind...I would name him Anqing," she answered, placing the bell back on its shelf.

Ryuga's ears perked up. "Anqing? I thought you despised him?"

"I did. But before that I loved him."

Ryuga sensed that she didn't need him to comment on her explanation, so he remained silent. He always suspected that Kiyohime regretted killing her lover, so he never felt the need to add to her guilt and torment by talking with her about it. Kiyohime continued to walk around her cave, picking up objects and setting them back where they belonged. She folded and unfolded a golden fan, opened and closed a lacquer box. Sighing, she held up a bronze birdcage to the firelight.

"I'm afraid I have nothing to offer a male hatchling as a gift," Kiyohime remarked, turning to face Ryuga. "Unless you were thinking of getting him a pet bird, that is."

"You don't need to worry about it. Perhaps you can just take the sword of that demon-slayer."

"Yes," Kiyohime said thoughtfully. "The sword of a demon-slayer would be perfect for your son. Come back on the next full moon, I'll have it by then."

Many days after his meeting with Kiyohime, he watched as the fragile paper fibers soaked and disintegrated in the small, fiercely moving whirlpool so out of place in the otherwise still lake. Ink smeared from the letter, destroying the words and therefore destroying all meaning and purpose they held.

Ryuga glared from his seat on the grass, turning a claw in tune with the whirlpool. How long had it been since a human had drowned in his waters? It had been a while since he had made his presence known to one of them, but he took some solace in the fact that most humans still knew better than to tread in his territory.

Ryuga dove and swam into his underwater grotto, the scales on his serpentine body flashing in the sunlight as he wove through the currents. Though he had thoroughly destroyed the letter, its contents still disturbed him.

The humans had gotten greedy, cunning and powerful in the last few centuries. No creature—tengu, yokai or even kirin—was safe from their industrious ambition.

This, of course, was a result of another bad choice; many of the immortals had made the decision to move to the spirit realm known as Reikai rather than try to coexist with the mortals when quite simply, they should have fought for their right to remain. Everyone had known that mortals were greedy. Why they hadn't been eradicated was a mystery to Ryuga.

His lover, so far across the sea, had written to tell him about a nest of dragon eggs destroyed close to where she resided. She was leaving the worldly plane and wanted him to follow.

The thought of being forced from his home lit his blood on fire with rage. He had spent centuries eating the bountiful supply of fish, tanning himself on the warm banks and occasionally taking to the skies if he felt the need for fresh air. This land was the only land he knew and he would not give it up.

If they left, his son would never know the world he came from. He would never see the rivers that ran like veins through the sacred grounds that Ryuga treasured. He would lose a part of his family's history, a part of his own self if he was raised in Reikai.

He remembered, so long ago, how humans would leave him offerings of fish and sweet fruits in hopes of gaining his favor. There were still offerings now and again, but they were few and far between. Humans preferred to worship each other—and themselves—these days.

These humans...they needed to be dealt with. Ryuga swam restlessly around his home, bits of rock falling slowly to the ground when he knocked into the walls. They needed to be shown that there were still magical creatures and that this land was for the immortals. Unfortunately, many dragons were pacifists; they ruled peacefully and quietly, preferring to avoid the humans rather than fight them.

So he decided to visit with Kiyohime, the only other

dragon he knew who had shed off her benign ways to fight for what was hers.

The transition between water and sky was nonexistent for Ryuga. He gracefully propelled himself through the water and shot into the air, his body like a black cloud dripping water to the earth below. He flew high enough that humans wouldn't be able to see him clearly, but low enough to make them wonder and hopefully fear.

"Kiyohime," he called out, landing gracefully outside of her cave. He couldn't smell her. "Kiyohime."

"You'll not find her here, Yamata."

Ryuga quickly turned at the calm, soft-spoken voice. Standing serenely on the top of a pile of rocks was a deer-like kirin, the curved horn on his forehead pointing directly at Ryuga.

Disbelief sunk into Ryuga's chest as the kirin regarded him. There were only two reasons the kirin ever showed themselves to anyone, even dragons. The first being a sign of prosperity. However, as the seconds passed and Kiyohime still hadn't arrived, Ryuga knew it had to be the other reason...

"She is no more," the kirin said.

The kirin had come to mark the passing of a great ruler.

163

Now that Ryuga had stopped, he could see that the trees drooped all around Kiyohime's domain, bowed in respect and sadness. The birds weren't chirping and not even a small semblance of wind blew through the area.

"She...perished?" The word didn't taste right on Ryuga's split tongue. The only other dragon that would fight, his only ally in a world where everyone else had given up. Gone.

"Death met her swiftly and mercilessly in the form of a wandering samurai."

"When?"

"Late last night. I can take you to her body, if you wish."

Ryuga considered it for a minute before nodding his head. The kirin pranced down the pile of rocks, his cloven hooves making no noise at all.

She was resting about an hour's walk down the river. Her bright green and red body was dazzling in the daylight. Her fine mane was knotted with blood, and her jaw looked crooked, misaligned with the top part of her face. A long, clean gash split her belly.

Ryuga stared at her body but still couldn't believe that a human had killed her. He stared at the gash, so precise it could have been the work of another dragon. Not a human.

A dragon. How could anything else have taken her life?

"Slaughtered," Ryuga breathed.

The kirin shook his head. "An incorrect assumption, my friend. The word would imply that she was a victim. An unfair term, when you consider that she initiated battle."

"If it was a human, she hardly had a choice. She deserved a better death than this." Ryuga snarled. He was unable to look away.

"Are you only now only able to see her pain? Her very existence was far more wretched than her death."

Ryuga thought back to the way Kiyohime seemed to drag herself throughout her cave, throughout her life. How she shyly asked for his company every few months and tried to hide her disappointment every time he left.

But this wasn't about her loneliness. This was about her murderer. If Ryuga had failed her as a friend while she lived, he would not fail her in death.

"Who did this?"

"Do not act in haste, dragon. You may be happier turning away from the very tragedy that marked Kiyohime's life. I tell you now that her fatal wound may have been the greatest gift she ever received."

Dragons were a proud, beautiful race. To think that any

165

of their kind would be better off slain by a human than alive was an opinion Ryuga couldn't accept. He exhaled slowly.

"A name, if you will, kirin."

"So you refuse to be swayed? Very well, if there is no stopping you, I will tell you. Her opponent was a mortal who goes by the pseudonym Sasayaki. But be aware of what truly drives you. Do you fight for justice or arrogance? Your decision shapes the world you bring your child into." The kirin turned and disappeared, leaving Ryuga with Kiyohime's corpse.

It wasn't the way of dragons to burn or bury their dead. Ryuga picked up her stiff body, her slender arms wrapped securely in his claws, and flew from the river that she used to spend her days gazing into. His arms became tired with her weight and he hated looking down because there was no way to see the earth below without seeing her face or the horrible, ugly gash.

He finally stopped when he reached the middle of the ocean. Gently, as if laying her on to a nest, he lowered her onto the ocean's surface and watched as the water embraced her. The still glimmering scales flashed like fireflies as the sunlight hit her. Her bloody mane floated about in a way that seemed whimsical and free. It almost looked like she was waving goodbye as she sunk to the ocean floor.

"Goodbye, my friend."

Sasayaki. The human word for whisper. Like a whisper he lingered in the back of Ryuga's mind, haunting his thoughts and his dreams for days on end. Like a whisper, there was very little information about him. Ryuga went to all of his sources, searching everywhere he could for even the smallest shred of fact. He found nothing.

So he was a little surprised when the information decided to come to him. Two weeks after Kiyohime's death, a tengu was perched high in a tree by Ryuga's grotto, whittling while he waited. When Ryuga hovered above the trees, he looked up.

"Well if it isn't Yamata himself. Wondered when you would show up," the tengu remarked, ruffling his feathers. Ryuga had always considered Tengu to be annoying, ugly little creatures. If he were a younger dragon, he might have killed him on sight, but desperation caused him to hesitate.

"What brings you to my domain, tengu?"

"You dragons have such bad social skills. No

welcomes? No pleasantries. Really quite rude in my opinion."

Ryuga's tail snapped behind him and thunder boomed in the sky. The tengu glanced up for a second and grinned, his long, long nose pointing to the streak of lightning.

"Let's not be so hasty, Yamata! That's no way to treat an ally."

"Explain yourself."

"Heard you were looking for someone. A human someone."

Ryuga's eyes narrowed. If the tengu was playing some sort of obnoxious joke, he would grab him by the neck and drown him on the way down to his grotto. Despite Ryuga's obvious impatience, the tengu continued with his uncouth manner of speaking.

"Ah, got your interest, huh? I can tell you anything you want to know about that Sasayaki fellow," the tengu offered, inspecting his whittling. "Go on, ask me anything."

"What do you have to gain from his death?"

"Really? Any question you want about the guy you've been searching weeks for and you ask about me? I'm flattered. Let's just say I have my own reasons and leave it at that, shall we?"

Ryuga didn't like the thought of being used, but he decided to ponder that later. He was too desperate to turn down any source, no matter how irritating it might have been.

"What does he look like?"

"He wears black armor with a red crane crest over his chest. But the armor isn't what you should be worried about. He carries a special sword. No one knows where he got it from or why it's so powerful, but it can slice through anything. Even dragon scales. But, you already know that, don't you?"

"Where is he now?" Ryuga cut in.

"Traveling westward, through the forest. He goes wherever us immortals kill humans then makes them drop like flies. Looks like he's out to make himself as some sort of savior for mankind. Disgusting."

"Why?"

"Revenge, I hear. His lover's heart was eaten by a powerful demon, and he's trying to attract his attention."

The samurai might not have gotten the demon's attention, but he had unfortunately gotten Ryuga's. For days, Ryuga stalked along the countryside, listening carefully for whispers of the demon-slayer. All the while

169

his heart hardened as he thought of Sasayaki, the nightmarish killer who left scarlet trails behind him. He may have been hailed as a hero by the humans, but he was despised and feared by everything else.

Finally, after days of searching, Ryuga caught up to the infamous warrior. He had set up camp by a riverside, but the forest bordering it was thick enough for Ryuga to hide and watch from. The samurai was tall by human standards, leaner than he was bulky. His skin was very pale, almost like the porcelain dolls that still lined Kiyohime's cave. Ryuga guessed it was from traveling and fighting by night rather than day.

He was a dainty thing, this Sasayaki. He held his sword carefully and walked quietly about his campsite. He was meticulous in the way he combed his silky hair, and Ryuga wondered if the same precision would be present in battle. For hours, Ryuga observed as he sat on a large rock and sharpened his sword. It flashed red and orange in the firelight.

Sasayaki stopped sharpening his blade and stared around the forest. Quickly, he stood and held his sword at the ready.

He never once called out into the darkness, never tried to

taunt his unseen enemy into attacking. He just stood quietly breathing, sword raised and listening as if the forest would tell him Ryuga's hiding place. Ryuga stayed completely still, confident that his black scales would blend seamlessly into the darkness. Sasayaki stayed just feet from where Ryuga stood hiding for a long moment before sheathing his sword and turning on his heel.

It would have been an opportune moment to strike.

Not yet, his instincts coaxed him. He had waited this long. He could be a little more patient.

For days he was like an ominous shadow, lurking in the trees and watching Sasayaki's every move. Every time Sasayaki killed, another image of Kiyohime's death would create itself in Ryuga's mind, and hate festered itself deep in the dragon's core.

Hate and...fear.

Sasayaki moved with the speed of the immortals, his sword nothing but a silvery blur while he sliced and wove through his battles. Every move was perfectly calculated. Every dodge perfectly timed. Ryuga was finally beginning to believe that a human—this human, at least—could have killed Kiyohime.

The samurai wasted no time after his kills. He simply

171

cleaned his blade, tended to his wounds and moved on as if nothing had happened.

The dragon wasn't sure he could defeat Sasayaki on his own. That sword of his thirsted for blood, and Sasayaki wouldn't turn a deaf ear to its needs. Though Ryuga was a great dragon, he was old, and not as fast as he used to be. Kiyohime had made the mistake of forgetting her weaknesses. He wouldn't do the same.

Because Kiyohime had to have gone into battle too arrogantly, not with a desire for death's cold touch. No self-respecting dragon—not even Kiyohime—would allow for a human to kill them. The kirin was wrong. Wrong about Kiyohime and wrong about him.

*Do you fight for justice or arrogance?*

A meaningless question posed by a creature that was too out of touch.

Ryuga had no intention of making his presence known, not even a second's notice. Sasayaki deserved to be hunted down the same way he hunted down immortals.

The sun was just about to set. The leaves sat still on the trees, no subtle breeze to shake them. Sasayaki would still be asleep for at least a little while longer. Ryuga's body moved in perfect synchronization with the wind, carrying him silently to the sleeping samurai.

This wasn't the first time that an enemy had come for Sasayaki while he slept. He slept on his back, fully dressed in his armor, his sword close at hand. As soon as Ryuga touched down he reached out for the sword. His claws wrapped around it at the same time that Sasayaki's hand did. His steely eyes had snapped open, and they were amazingly clear for someone who had just awakened.

Ryuga was stronger, but Sasayaki was more familiar with his weapon. He twisted it out of the dragon's claws and rolled a good distance away, straightening up and facing his opponent. He studied Ryuga for a few seconds, but whatever he was planning wasn't clear on his solemn face.

Sasayaki lunged, feigning left but striking right. A hairline scratch appeared on Ryuga's jaw as Sasayaki struck again.

Watching him and fighting him were two different things. As a spectator, Ryuga had thought that Sasayaki's movements were mechanical, without feeling and a result of well-thought out battle plans. But that couldn't be. He moved like a whirlwind, wild yet completely controlled. Sasayaki's sword against Ryuga's talons. Red streaks ran across Ryuga's arms. Bits of Sasayaki's leather armor broke off, soaked in blood. Sasayaki thrust his sword into Ryuga's chest, and the dragon hissed in pain, trying to think through the loud ringing that filled his ears. Sasayaki drove the sword in deeper, indifferent to the blood that sprouted from the open wound.

Darkness lined the edges of Ryuga's vision. He was going to lose his lands. Dragons would cite him as another example of why they should give up and leave. His own son wouldn't know him the same way he hadn't known his own father. He would die and his carcass would rot for weeks, forgotten and forsaken in the middle of the forest.

No.

He would not die as Kiyohime had.

Arms shaking, he grabbed the blade, yanked it out of his body and ripped it from the Samurai's hands. It landed too far for Sasayaki to be able to recover. Ryuga licked the blood from his claws. The warrior without his sword was helpless. It was time for him to pay for his transgressions.

Sasayaki was quick, but his stamina was only that of a human's. Ryuga was stronger, and it was only after a few missed hits that he ripped the front portion of Sasayaki's armor off. Immediately, he clawed a hole into the samurai's

shoulder socket, watching with satisfaction as blood
spread like a blossoming flower on the white fabric.

Sasayaki clenched his teeth and tried to take a step back,
but Ryuga elbowed him in the jaw, sending him twirling to
land face-down into the hard dirt. He tore the helmet from
his head and dug his claws into the back of Sasayaki's
neck, dragging down to the small of his back, leaving four
jagged lines in their wake. He pressed down hard before
retracting them. Through the torment the warrior stayed
silent, trembling and trying his best to curl into himself.

Then, with a daring he hadn't expected, Sasayaki turned
on his back and stabbed Ryuga's cheek. The second,
hidden sword wasn't as powerful as the first, but the scales
on Ryuga's face weren't as strong as the ones on his body.
Rivulets of blood streamed from the new wound and Ryuga
howled in pain as Sasayaki crawled towards his sword.

With savage strength, Ryuga rushed forward and
grabbed Sasayaki's head and bashed it into the ground,
picking it up with enough strength to bend his neck back
before slamming it into the dirt. He repeated for several
minutes until most of the rage had faded. Blood loss was
making him dizzy, he had to finish this battle, or it would
turn into a murder-suicide. Taking a breath, he stared down

at the unmoving body beneath him.

"You know, I spent a good deal of time thinking," Ryuga mused, circling around the fallen warrior. "I couldn't decide if I wanted to rip off your head or drown you. But those are both too quick, too easy. I want you to suffer the way you forced everyone else to suffer. I want the creatures you would have destroyed to come rip the skin off of your screaming face."

"No!" Sasayaki screamed, willing himself to his knees, his eyes closed against the flow of blood creeping out from his hair. He managed to wipe his face on his sleeve. He glared up at the dragon.

"I refuse to die yet. I've come too close."

"How amusing!" Ryuga intoned, a dry laugh crawling out of his throat. "You've had no problem destroying the immortals, but now when your time has come, you complain? You're pathetic. You ought to know when to stay down and graciously accept death." With a lazy swipe of his tail, Ryuga sent him back to the ground.

Sasayaki cried out as he hit the dirt. His breath rattled in his lungs and he choked as blood splashed over his lips. Ryuga sauntered over and dug his claws into the human's chest. He had expected to feel some sort of satisfaction

176

from the scream that ripped its way out of Sasayaki's mouth, but he felt nothing. Ryuga had behaved as a wild animal before, but his calm demeanor had found its way back to him. He found that he didn't want to make the human scream. He just wanted him disposed of.

"W-why?" Sasayaki rasped out, wheezing from the effort of speaking.

*Do you fight for justice or arrogance?*

Ryuga paused. Why would it matter to Sasayaki what his reasons were? The warrior was about to die. There was nothing he could do with the information. Had he still been full of malice, he might have liked the thought of Sasayaki dying without an answer. But there was no chance of Sasayaki surviving, and he decided he could afford to grant a last request to someone was about to lose everything.

"Because, human, you are a threat. You killed one of the strongest dragons in the East. You threaten my entire race and our future. Your motives might have been pure at one point—they might still be pure—but anyone can be corrupted. I cannot place my future on something as uncertain as your mindset or morality. Your life is a small price to pay for the security of my family, Sasayaki."

He retracted his claws and turned away from the

doomed warrior, bloody paw prints following him to the sword that could no longer help its master. Cackles and rustling feathers could be heard among the foliage.

"Heh, you're the best, Yamata," the familiar crow of the tengu remarked from the shadows. "We can take it from here."

Night would close in quickly on the fallen samurai. Ryuga wiped blood—his own blood—from the blade before taking to the skies.

Ryuga clenched his bleeding chest as he flew back to his cove. The water would help soothe his wounds.

The blood spread and dispersed around him as he sunk into the water. By now the samurai would be no more than bones picked clean. How odd to think that just mere hours ago he had slept so peacefully.

Ryuga curled into himself, finally ready to relax. Sasayaki's blood-smeared face loomed before Ryuga's closed eyes. Despite his intense hatred for the human, he couldn't help but grudgingly respect his pride and determination.

He thought of the egg that was waiting for him in the west, of the sword he would present to his son when the time was right. He would teach his son that sometimes, fighting was the only way. And he would tell the story of Sasayaki to remind him that nothing could ever hope to defy a dragon, so long as there was a comrade to avenge him.

He would have much to do to prepare for his journey. He settled into a more comfortable position. If Kiyohime could finally rest, so could he.

# The Dragon's Clause

*Kelly A. Harmon*

He had to hurry.

Giuseppe Piccoli, San Marino's attorney, took the two hundred silver *soldi* collected from the citizens and poured them from the collection box into his rucksack. His fingers shook, and a sweat broke out on his brow even as his stomach roiled. But what was he to do? His debt grew larger the longer he could not pay. And now they threatened the life of his children.

This would solve all his problems, and the city lost nothing.

For more than three hundred years the city threw away the coins collected for the sacrifice offered during the Founder's Day festivities. Today, these garbage coins would help him and his family survive. The custom angered him, tossing good money down a well when it could be used for so much more.

Outside the *Consiglio Grande e Generale Municipio* he could hear the revelers in the street.

*Merda.* He had to hurry.

The sun barely crested the horizon of Monte Titano, and some were drunk already. Where were the *balesrieri*, the crossbowmen?

Preparing for the annual contest of course. They would be of almost no use to the republic today while they preened for the crowds and vied for the honor of being the best bowman. None would be standing guard this day.

Perhaps he could use their preoccupations to his advantage. So busy with their own importance and today's contest, it's possible his early visit to the municipal building would go unnoticed. He could only hope, for his daughters' sake.

From his rucksack, he pulled a bulging cloth parcel: his winter scarf, the four corners tied together to hold the contents. Two flicks of his thumbs and the knot unraveled, revealing a cache of small stones. None was bigger than his thumbnail, the size of a silver *soldi*. He lifted the edge of a red silk bag and thrust the stones in by the handful.

When enough stones filled the bag, Giuseppe tied it off with a cloth-of-gold ribbon and put the bag in the safe. The *Capitani Reggenti* would sacrifice it to San Marino's dragon later in the day.

181

The silk bag tumbled end over end down the dry well, once or twice hitting the natural stone sides of the chute until it landed with a *clink* on top of a large pile of gold and silver coins, then rolled down the heaped mound to bump into the grey-green scales of a dragon's thigh.

"At last," the dragon breathed, two tendrils of smoke rising out of his nostrils as gently as the first curls of steam from a teapot set to boil. He lifted his large head from slumber and blinked away the sleep.

Salga di Alato stretched his neck, craning it back almost far enough to touch his raised wings.

He extended one foot to hook the bag with a claw and drew it close. He held the heavy bag with his front feet, massaging it. Then with a jerk of one hooked nail, he undid the ribbon and upturned the sack with the other. Two hundred stones clanked against the metal and precious gems which made up his hoard.

"This can't be," he said, riffling through the pile, turning up stone after stone in his precious pile of coins. "Surely the people of San Marino are not trying to cheat me?"

He sat down on his haunches, puffing great clouds of smoke, as he surveyed the pile. "With whom do they think they are dealing?"

He thrust the silk bag away from him. With an uncontrollable bellow, he tipped his head back and sucked in a convulsive breath. He bent his head forward and roared in fury, spitting forth a stream of fire.

The cave lit up, revealing the humble abode of a dragon. The mound of gold and silver coins, priceless gemstones and objects d'art towered almost as high as the municipal building of San Marino. Even with a dragon sitting atop it, the large cave could have held two or even three times more.

"How dare they!" he said, white smoke still roiling.

He decided he would give the Sanmariners an opportunity to make amends. They've fulfilled their part of the bargain for more than three hundred years, after all. This had to be a mistake. If not....well, he could set them right.

Salga nodded his head thoughtfully, his anger cooling. Only the barest wisps of smoke tickled his nose. Taking a calming breath, he relaxed, calling on the air elements to help him formulate his shift to human shape.

He unfurled his wings for balance and stood on hind legs, the length of his long, scaled tail holding the brunt of his weight, keeping the ponderous body upright. Once balanced, he said the words of *change*.

He felt the magic first at the crown of his head, tiny pinpoints of light dancing on the ridge of his skull. It tingled, sending pleasant little shocks across his neck and along the length of his spine. Downward the magic sang through his veins, light gamboling across his scales, until it reached his clawed feet and the tip of his tail. The large dragon shimmered, refulgent in the glow of the flickering light. The light swelled and blinked out, soap-bubble like, and the dragon disappeared.

In his place, standing at the edge of a mound of gold stood a handsome man wearing a gray-green tunic and trousers. He bent to the pile and retrieved a ruby ring and a heavy, gold necklace with links as thick as fingers. The pendant, half the size of his human fist, depicted a flying dragon. Fashioned by some Greek artisan centuries ago, it meant nothing to him, but it usually impressed those he met when he masqueraded as a human. He donned the necklace and the ring, the latter on the third finger of his right hand. Salga smiled as the metal warmed to his touch, as if it became a part of him.

He climbed the pile, as tall as three men, and retrieved the stones, human fingers sorting the fraudulent from the authentic with the speed of a dragon's innate skill. He needed neither sight nor tactile sense to pluck the dross from gold but sensed the stones as his hands passed near. In moments, he filled the silk bag and tied it closed with the cloth-of-gold ribbon. With a sigh, he made his way to the front of the cave and the winding road that led up the Appenines and its highest peak, Monte Titano.

Salga di Alato arrived at the Grand and General Council Municipal building shortly before *terce*. Perfect, he thought, he could meet with the city representatives before they broke for their midday meal.

"I've come to speak with the *Capitani Reggenti*," he told the *segretario*. "Either one, or both. It matters not."

The lighting was dim inside the *municipio*, but Salga could make out the historical paintings on the far wall. Too bad one did not depict himself, he thought. There would be far less misunderstanding here if they included him within their history.

Two armored men stood equidistant from the secretary's desk, close enough to help if there were need but far enough away to stay out of council business.

"Have you an appointment?" the secretary asked,

looking down at his calendar then back at Salga.

*Un idiota* could see the *segretario* thought he had no appointment.

"I have a standing appointment with the *Capitani Reggenti*. It concerns our contract business."

The secretary's eyes widened, then he cracked a smile. "You jest. The only standing appointment permitted on the books is with—"

"The agent of San Marino's dragon." It was Salga's turn to smile. He held up the necklace. "I am he."

A brief moment of silence passed before the secretary erupted in a full belly laugh. "I will share this with the *Consiglio*," he said, wiping his eyes. "They will have a good laugh, too." He smiled again at Salga. "Do you have a petition to drop off or need information? Perhaps there is something else I can help you with?"

"You can help me with facilitating the *terce* appointment," Salga said. "By the dragon's contract with San Marino, I have the right to request the next meeting time on the calendar. I am requesting it."

The secretary looked down at his books.

"There is a full council meeting at *terce*," the secretary said. "And then they break for lunch. I cannot–"

Salga felt himself losing patience. Perhaps he should have exercised this right more often over the years. "Were you not apprised of your duties when you were sworn in?"

"Three-hundred-year-old fairy tales do not a duty make," said the secretary. He turned to the guard at his right. "If you please."

The guard lifted his glaive and took a step toward the desk.

The council chamber door opened and two men stepped out, the *Capitani Reggenti:* Pietro Della Baldi and Vincenzo Refi.

Pietro said, "What is going on here?"

"This man says he's an agent for San Marino's dragon."

Silence greeted his announcement. Then in unison, the Captains Regent looked at each other and laughed, then looked back at the secretary and Salga as if expecting them to join in.

A moment passed.

Pietro Della Baldi ran a hand through his graying hair and shrugged, looking at Refi. "The dragon's agent desires a meeting. So meet we must." He pulled the door of the council chamber open wide. "Come in, sir, and let us spend a few moments talking about the dragon's desires."

Salga couldn't tell if Capitani Della Baldi humored him or believed him. It mattered not. He was getting his audience.

Della Baldi turned to Refi. "Do you mind if we adjourn to my office?"

Refi shook his head. "We'll be more comfortable."

"Let the council know we're adjourned until after lunch."

They walked through the council hall and through another door at the rear. Not much had changed in the two hundred or so years since he had been here last, Salga thought. The rooms were still dim, still furnished with dark woods, still waxed and polished to a sheen. The white paint on the walls didn't do enough to brighten the style of the ancient building.

Della Baldi's office told another story. A large window dominated one side of the room, sending in a bright shower of light. Here, too, the room was painted white, but the light intensified it. A diary lay open on his desk, a quill and ink jar to the left of it. The day's outgoing correspondence lay stacked to the right, the red wax seal of the *Capitani Reggenti* declaring them official notices of the court.

Evidently, Della Baldi didn't entrust the *segretario* with such tasks. So who did he and Refi trust to make certain the dragon's tribute was paid?

Della Baldi gestured to two chairs in front of his desk and waited for both Salga and Refi to sit before seating himself. "So you are the dragon's emissary," he said, eyebrows raised. "It's been quite some time since he's sent his agent to the people of San Marino."

Refi scooted his chair around to face Salga. *Allying himself with Della Baldi*, Salga thought. Unusual that he would do so, since they wore badges belonging to opposing political parties.

Refi thrust out his chin, accusing. "Do you have proof you come from the dragon?"

"I knew it would come to that," Salga said. "I have already shown you my seal, but you will also be interested in *this*." He reached into his tunic and brought out the red silk bag, laying it on Della Baldi's desk.

Refi stood, pushing his chair back with such force that it tumbled over. "Where did you get that?"

Salga turned his head toward Refi, "From the dragon, of course... *capasci?*"

"No, I don't understand," Della Baldi said. "Is the

dragon rejecting our tribute this year?"

"*Si*, in a way," Salga said. He pushed the bag forward on the desk. "Open it."

Della Baldi looked at Refi, who shrugged. It was slight, but Salga had had six hundred years to learn to read humans. He did not mistake the gesture. Clearly, the two had united against him. It was a shame, because he had hoped to use their opposing political viewpoints to his advantage. He knew the missing money would make things worse between him and the city...and Della Baldi and Refi *were* the city.

Della Baldi untied the ribbon and dumped the contents of the bag on his desk.

"Dio! Where has the money gone? San Marino gave two hundred *soldi* to the dragon this year."

"No, *Reggente*, they did not. They gave him two hundred *sasso*. And someone went through a great deal of trouble to make sure each stone was similar in shape and size. This smacks of fraud, and the dragon is very unhappy." He offered the two of them a grim smile.

"You are the fraud," Refi said, pointing a finger at Salga. "San Marino has paid tribute and you have come here to steal from us again."

"Again?" Salga asked.

"Yes, again," Refi said. "You obviously took the first two hundred *soldi*, and now you expect us to give you another two hundred by telling us you are the dragon's agent. Be gone." He turned to Della Baldi, who nodded. "Leave, before we throw you in jail for the imposter you are."

"Your grandfathers' grandfathers' grandfathers and the dragon created a binding contract." Salga said. "If you fail to act on it, San Marino will fall."

"San Marino will never fall," said Refi.

"You place a great deal of faith in your *balesrieri*, *Reggente* Refi. They may be able to hold the walls against an invading army from below, but can they seal this city from the air? I guarantee you San Marino's legendary crossbowmen cannot keep a dragon from your ramparts."

Della Baldi stood. "Please leave, sir. It is better for you to go now, then for us to take you away."

Salga nodded. Della Baldi looked sad, as though he regretted asking him to leave. It was Refi who thought him insane, or worse, truly believed him to be a thief. Della Baldi put on a united front. Salga turned to him.

"There are a great many visitors still in San Marino for

191

the festival," he said. "Are you certain you want to risk their lives?"

A long moment passed. Della Baldi nodded. "Please go now."

"I am instructed to tell you, as the dragon's agent," Salga said, "that the dragon himself will visit San Marino. You will not like the outcome." He turned and left the chamber, crossing the anteroom and nodding to the *segretario* on his way out.

Salga exited the high-walled gate of the city and walked the dirt road down Monte Titano to his lair. He hated that this had to be done, but a contract was a contract, after all.

*Where* diplomazia *fails, strength prevails*, he thought, entering the cave.

He took off the ring and the necklace. Standing on tiptoe, he called on the magic of the air and changed back. Lethargy stole over him as he climbed to the top of his hoard. Taking human form consumed so much of his energy. His eyes closed and he burrowed his belly into the coin, feeling the coolness of it against his scales. Sighing, he lay his great head down on his front claws and settled into slumber. Tomorrow, approaching midday when the crowds were likely to be their thickest, he would exercise his rights of the contract.

The day dawned clear and cool. As the first rays of sun crept into Salga's dark lair, the dragon stirred awake. He swept his large tail back and forth then wrapped it around himself, sending an avalanche of coins rushing down his hoard of gold and silver. He could almost imagine a waterfall, the slithering coins shushing against each other until they stopped at the bottom, tinkling against the bare stone floor.

After a few moments, he stood, causing another barrage of coins to fall with every movement, first arching his back down like a sway-backed horse, then up like a spitting cat, shaking out his leather wings in unison. He couldn't unfurl them in the tight confines of the cave, but soon, when he made his way back to San Marino in true form, he would have the luxury of stretching them wide.

It's a shame, he thought, but not wholly unexpected. This new generation considered the contract legend, not truth. They would learn, and perhaps the next would benefit.

He stepped down from the tremendous pile toward the cave opening, each foot sinking ankle deep into coins, just like a walk on a beach, and just as pleasurable. Sunlight caught him on the crown of his head, warming him. He sniffed the air, enjoying the tang of wood smoke, watching the sun creep higher into the sky.

The orb lit the hillside with its brilliant dawning, but at this hour, shadows still bathed San Marino. He sat down on his haunches and waited.

Down the mountainside, flocks of sheep grazed on the elevated hillocks, looking like white, puffy ants. He could smell their pungent odor rising on an updraft. To the east, winter crops had been sown, but he could still see the fertile, black soil of the fields.

Salga waited at the lip of his cave, watching the mountainside and her inhabitants wake to the new day. Finally, the sun reached a point where its rays crested the walls of even Monte Titano.

The dragon leapt from the mouth of his cave, unfurled his wings, and dove down the shear side of the mountain, reveling in the air blowing in his face, the warmth of sunshine percolating under his scales and the buoyancy of flight. It had been so long since he'd been out in the daytime, he'd nearly forgotten the pleasure of it. Flipping his belly to the heat of the sun, Salga caught an updraft and

194

turned, beating his heavy wings. He shot past the walls of San Marino, rising even higher on the wind. The sun still warmed the parts of him it touched, but the wind chilled him, slowed the beating of his wings, hardened his heart.

He leveled off and angled his nose downward toward the wide plateau which formed the city of San Marino, looking for the town square. He meant to invoke fear and panic as he swept over the main thoroughfare, gliding low and fast, casting a dark shadow as his immense body passed over.

As he imagined, crowds filled the main street and its smaller tributaries. Hundreds of people milled in the road, laughing, playing games, watching the crossbow tourney. A herd of drinkers spilled out from under a red-and-white awning, mugs and goblets overflowing in the noonday sun.

Salga found his anger climbing. *Puny humans,* he thought, daring to celebrate the founding of a fortress which they held only by his own generosity. They couldn't remember, even with their collective memories, the bargain they made with him. He had to swallow back the steam building in his throat or be consumed by it himself. Instead of letting loose the fire stoked in his breast, he tamped it down and unleashed a strident call as he approached the city.

The cry caught the revelers' attention, and they turned to face him. Salga opened his great wings and glided downward, skimming over their heads, savoring the horrified looks on their faces. They ran like sheep, bleating their fear, stampeding over one another to get to safety. Their screams echoed across the mountaintop, Salga thought, and he hadn't harmed a single one.

At the end of the city square, where a wall prevented Sanmariners from falling to their death down the cliff face, Salga caught another updraft and used it to propel himself higher. He pumped his wings, hearing the leathern creak with each downward thrust. Now he would teach them about forgetfulness.

He dived.

Gulping air on the way down, he stoked the fire that lived within him.

As he got closer to the city, he saw a line of *balesrieri* pull back their bow strings and loose their arrows. Several found their mark. He cried out again, an uncontrolled bellow encompassing both his pain and his rage.

He flew over the city, swooping down over one large tower, and set fire to the roofs of the *municipio*, the barracks and a series of smaller buildings in his path toward

196

the second of the three towers.

There, several *balesrieri* managed to reach the ballista. They cranked it high and ratcheted the bowstring back, loading a large, steel bolt into the slot. Ere he could react, they fired the bolt, and reached for their crossbows. Salga roared, letting loose a stream of fire onto the ballista.

Agony ripped through the leather webbing of his right wing as the bolt drilled a ragged hole in his flesh. The hammer blow of it forced his wing back and he fell nearly to the ground before the weak pumping he managed between the debilitating injury and the pain of it saved him from crashing to the cobblestone. He rose, heavy and ponderous, until he found a buoyant wind to support him. The crossbowmen fired their weapons again.

He twisted around, protecting his softer belly from the bolts, jerking from pain where the arrows managed to sink into flesh. Most bounced from his hardened scales like rainwater.

Still, the pain tempted him to set fire to the entire city, to kill as many as he could, but he stifled the urge. Without the city, he had no tribute, and this was about money, after all.

When he was high enough to control a glide, he circled

the city once more, then descended back to his lair. Late into the night, he could hear the sounds of the citizens rallying to douse the fires and help the injured. Finally, silence fell where there should have been gaiety.

Salga plucked the crossbow bolts one by one from his hide.

Giuseppe Piccoli filled his pockets with the few remaining *soldi* and made his way to the square. He knew he had to do this, yet it frightened him more than anything he had ever done. Indeed, it might cost him his life, which still might be for naught. What was the use of stealing in order to save the lives of his family if they might yet be killed by the dragon?

He tied the rope around the dry well and lowered himself down. The small, covered lantern he carried illuminated the shaft enough for him to see moss growing in tufts on the walls, and various lines where the water had rested at some point before retreating, and finally, the light disappeared into the darkness of the large cavern.

After a few moments, he saw the lantern light glint off something shiny below him.

His heart began to beat as fast as hummingbird wings.

Heat rushed to his face and he began to sweat. He slid the remaining few feet to the pile of gold on hands too damp to keep his weight on the rope.

He landed with a jarring thump, sending a shower of coins rushing down the hill of gold.

"Who dares to enter my home?" Salga asked, resting only a few feet away. He ached, and he was in no mood for confrontation.

The lamplight brightened.

Salga watched a man, so afraid of speaking his entire body shook. He moved the lantern's hood back to shed more light, then sat down, shaking, on the pile.

"G-g-g-iuseppe P-p-piccoli," he said. "I've come to make amends."

"I thought for certain the *Reggenti* would send a knight to try to kill me." Salga looked him up and down. "You don't look capable of a fight."

"I'm not a knight, sir. I'm an attorney." His voice still trembled.

Salga raised his massive head and turned toward Giuseppe, who fell back on his hands, as if expecting the dragon to take a snap at him. Salga said, "If you're not here to try to kill me, why are you here?"

Giuseppe sat up, pushing a few coins and gems down the side of the pile as he righted himself. "I'm the one who took your silver. Please don't punish the city for my actions."

"You're a brave man to come here and admit that."

Giuseppe shook his head, swallowing so hard, Salga could see his Adam's apple fall and rise above his collared tunic. "I'm a pathetic man. I didn't want to come here today, but I knew I needed to. If there were only me to consider, I would have left well enough alone, but I have to think about my children and the people of San Marino."

Salga nodded. "Why did you take the silver?"

"I needed the money."

"There are other means to obtain money."

"Not so much and so easily. I had promised to pay off an agreement by Founder's Day. I didn't have the money, but I had means to obtain the city's."

Tiny curls of smoke drifted out of Salga's nostrils. He turned his head to the side and snorted, a tiny flame escaping. Giuseppe blanched white in the lantern light.

Salga said, "You sacrificed the honor of San Marino by paying your own debts first?"

His voice a whisper, Giuseppe said, "It wasn't like that."

"No?"

"No," he said, wiping the palms of his hands across the tops of his knees. "For hundreds of years the city has collected money and thrown it away—"

"It is rent, Signor Piccoli, no matter how the city has popularized it with festivities and tournaments."

"But no one alive has ever seen you. What are we to think? To us, it's just throwing money away." He made a gesture of throwing something down on the ground.

Salga heaved a deep sigh. These words confirmed what he thought all along.

Giuseppe said, "I beg you not to harm the people of San Marino. I'm the one at fault. Kill me, if you have to, but please leave the city alone." He dug in his pocket and retrieved the remaining *soldi*. With cupped hands, he held thirteen silver coins out to Salga. "Here is what remains of the tribute after I've paid my debt. I swear I've not kept a single one back."

"Yet you are still in my debt for over a hundred and eighty *soldi*."

"I owe the city," said Giuseppe.

201

"No, you owe me," said Salga. "After all, the money you took represented rent San Marino owes me." He huffed a stream of smoke straight up through his nostrils.

An idea formed.

"What price would you pay for stealing from the city?"

Giuseppe hung his head. "I would lose my position as city attorney. My family would be shamed and need to leave San Marino." He drew in a deep breath. "My right hand would be chopped off at the wrist and I would go to debtor's prison until my family could raise the funds to pay off the debt and the interest incurred while the city waited to be paid."

Salga nodded his giant head and then lowered it, resting it upon his front claws.

After much consideration, he realized that the problem was not San Marino, but himself. His contract with the town was short-sighted. Although his kind is accustomed to living long lives and remembering the ages, he could not expect as much from these short-lived humans.

The fault lay with him.

He possessed a contract with forgetful beings. If not Giuseppe, it would have been someone else forgetting his existence and stealing his rents. And if he didn't find a solution to the problem now, it would continue over and over again.

He rose up on his front legs, looking down at Giuseppe who still shook with fear.

"Be thankful you owe your debt to me, Giuseppe Piccoli—"

"I am a dead man," he said, crossing himself.

"Nothing so harsh," said Salga, feeling the pain of a bolt hole in his wing. "I find I am in need of an attorney."

He pawed through the pile of gold, precious gems and jewelry until he found the heavy gold necklace with the dragon emblem and handed it over to Giuseppe. "You're now my agent," he said. "I demand complete honesty and fair representation."

Giuseppe stared at the heavy badge of office, clearly stunned. Salga continued to tickle the pile with his claws, sorting money. The Sanmariner coins should have been mostly on the top, but his hoard had been repeatedly disturbed over the last few days. He sorted a few smaller denominations from the side of the pile and handed those over to Giuseppe who asked, "And how am I to perform for you?"

"Take these coins and purchase supplies for writing:

materials sound enough not to deteriorate for hundreds of years. We are amending my contract with the city." He lowered himself back to the pile, taking care not to jar the injured wing.

Giuseppe raised his brows. "You think the city will agree?"

"Of course. I'm offering them a better deal," said the dragon, sweeping his tail around to warm his feet.

"The council has approved the new contract," Pietro Della Baldi said. "It only remains for the three of us to sign it."

Vincenzo Refi took the heavy document from Della Baldi's hands and read the words himself, as if reading them could make them any more believable. "This is real?" he asked Giuseppe Piccolo.

"The dragon dictated the words himself," Giuseppe said. "You can see the contract is written in my hand. And here," he held up the large, dragon pendant on the gold chain. "You see I now carry his seal."

Della Baldi had his arms crossed on his chest, one hand raised to stroke his chin. "It seems too good to be true," he said. "For the same terms of rent he has always received, the dragon promises to defend the city from all invaders as long as he shall live. And when he chooses a mate and has children, he can promise their loyalty to the city until his daughters leave to reside with their chosen mates or his sons move away to collect their own hoards."

"Imagine," said Giuseppe, an excited smile brightening his face, "in a matter of time you will have an army of dragons defending San Marino. Our city shall never fall."

"He does require that we allow him to participate in the Founders Day Festival every twentieth year," said Refi, laying the contract on the table.

"It is nothing," said Giuseppe. "He only wants that San Marino doesn't forget him again."

"Reasonable," said Della Baldi. "Reminding the city of his presence can only help us avoid... *misunderstandings*."

He turned to Refi. "I'm ready to sign. Do you agree?"

Refi nodded and picked up a quill.

Della Baldi signed his own name then asked Giuseppe. "I'm curious why a dragon even collects money. After all, where could he spend it?"

Giuseppe smiled. "He doesn't collect just money. You should see the cave. He has gold and silver, jewelry, even gemstones and precious-metal art."

"It seems like a waste," Refi said, signing his own name.

205

"I agree that paying rent seems reasonable enough, but Pietro is right. And what good is art to a dragon? Can he even appreciate it?"

Giuseppe rolled his copy of the contract and tucked it away. "Dragons hoard their riches until there is enough to weave into a nest and impress a prospective mate. Once our dragon has enough to woo a spouse, he'll settle down and rear that army he promised us."

"And has our dragon begun weaving his nest?" Refi asked.

"No," said Giuseppe, shaking his head. "He simply keeps it piled. Perhaps when we're all doddering he may have enough to begin weaving."

Della Baldi looked at Refi, but he asked Giuseppe, "So offering him more gold or silver will encourage him to mate sooner?"

"That seems likely."

Della Baldi turned to Refi. "Perhaps we can afford to be more generous in our rent. After all, our payment has not changed in over two centuries." Refi was nodding in agreement before Della Baldi could even finish his statement. "In fact, it appears our dragon has been very generous to us. I think we could do no less for him."

Giuseppe coughed, hiding a smile behind his hand.

"We can easily double our present payment," Della Baldi said, watching Refi continue to nod. "And we can add a clause to revisit the payment schedule at a later date."

"That's very generous of you," Giuseppe said, pulling another contract from his satchel and spreading it on the table. "I think you'll see this contract includes the very same terms you've named, and we can write in the new rental payment." He looked into two sets of surprised eyes and shrugged. "Salga anticipated that you might consider offering more if you knew what it could buy you."

Giuseppe watched the *Capitani Reggenti* sign the new contract and placed his own signature below theirs. He sanded the ink to hurry it dry, then rolled up the scroll to take with him. He left the *municipio* and crossed the small square to the other side of the city.

Shadows covered San Marino as the sun fell below the horizon.

He walked to the third tower of San Marino, the one with no doorway for entry, and stepped into the darkest shadow where the high wall of the city met the stone of the tower. Pressing his hands against two separate bricks, he pushed, releasing a spring mechanism and opening a small door inward.

He entered and closed the door to a room tinier than the tower was wide. A staircase led down below the city. On his way to see Salga, he reflected that there would be no more trips down a dry well to meet his patron, and with a little luck, he'd be godfather to a dragon whelp before he confessed his sins before God himself.

# Lizard Claw

*E.A. Fow*

"Stay still!"

"Stay there!"

I don't want to stay still, and I will not stay here.

"Stay there!" she shouts at me, louder this time. I am not
sure who died and made her lord of the plains, but she has
always been this way, and as she is standing up waving her
sword and I am not. I have decided I'll stay here. When she
moves her foot off my head, perhaps I will change my
mind.

I hear the screeching and cover my ears then close my
eyes, too, for good measure. If I curl up tightly enough,
even if the lizard gets her, perhaps it will not realize I am
here at all.

Her foot mashes down against my head, and I worry she
has heard my thoughts somehow. She can do everything
else; why couldn't she read minds? Then I realize she's not
punishing me, just steeling herself for what is to come. The
cries of the lizard grow louder and angrier, and I can almost
catch meaning in the hissing, squealing, multi-tonal

discord. I can almost hear language, and I realize the lizard is not angry at all; he is not in control of what he is doing—he is impelled. Then I feel her thrashing above me. Her foot lifts off my head, and I am suddenly freed, so I curl up tighter, and then her foot stamps back down, and I can feel her rocking above me, wrestling with something, slashing with her arms, the turmoil of the battle transmitted through her into me, and suddenly I am sprayed with blood and the world smells like sulfur.

I passed out.

I only know because she nudges me with her foot, gently this time. When I open my eyes, she is standing above me, the lizard's clawed foot, huge and gnarled, is swinging from her right hand. Her sword stands vertical in the soft earth, swaying triumphant.

"How is it I have to fight with lizards and you get to nap?" Then she prods my face with the back of a horny claw, not the point, which could disfigure me. She wields the huge foot as if it is nothing.

When we walk back to the village, she can't stop talking about the fight. I have to carry the damned lizard's amputated foot while she swaggers and feints and practices the victory speech she will never make. She doesn't notice the smoke rising in the distance or react to the dots in the air that get larger and larger as they fly towards us. It's not until the lizards' dreadful screeching begins that her muscles tense and she takes a proper grip on her sword. We stand completely still, but there is no chance they haven't seen us with their huge, glittering eyes. The only chance they won't fly towards us is if they have other plans. Lizards are old, all of them. Even the young ones are old, and they don't change their minds easily. It means we don't always have to run when we see them. Usually they can't be bothered with mere Plainsmen, but if their eyes are trained on us, there will be a fight or a death or burning. It is madness we have to hunt them, but when the village runs low on marrow salve or weapons, it has to be done. If she wasn't the lizard reaper, we would never be out in the open plain by ourselves. Perhaps they are coming to punish us for what we have just done. The hard won foot is still dripping, and she is still sweating from the fight. I can barely breathe, waiting, waiting, and they grow bigger, now the size of sparrows in the distance, and then robins, and then it is clear they are coming our way. I look at her and then at the ground; should I crouch now or will we run to a better position? She shakes her head at me.

"We need to keep walking," she says. "They'll come to us, so we should keep walking, there's no point in letting them make us late."

I admire her hubris, but our inevitable meeting with the lizards makes my privates shrink in fear. Still, I obey, I always obey her. It is the only reason I have lived this long, and I never thought I would get to sixteen at all. We walk towards the village, still a mile away, and I see the smoke is still rising, not a blanket of it—the lizards have not flamed it—but a single column rising towards the azure sky.

The screeching grows louder, and again I almost hear words in it. I sense alarm, not hunger or anger or sport. She turns to me now.

"Give me the foot," she says. Not even the talons, not even the claws, just *the foot* as if it is nothing. I hand the heavy thing to her. It has stopped dripping its sulfurous blood now, but its stink clings to me. Before I can wonder why she wants to carry it, she twirls it by its ankle stump and swings it up into the air, holding it above her like a flaming torch. Its dead claws glint, and the screeching turns to shrieks. The lizards look the size of game birds now, but their shrieking fills the entire world, and the ground vibrates. I fear my eardrums will burst and I fall to the

212

ground covering them. She, however, stands shaking the huge lizard claw like an angry fist.

*Look what I will do to you*, she says without speech. *Look what will become of you.*

The screeching stops, and now it is their beating wings that fill the air. It gusts around us as they approach, and I wonder if she will throw me to them this time, a snack to pacify them, as she has threatened in moments of great annoyance. Instead, she shakes the gnarled foot one more time and turns her back on them, reaching down to pull me up and away with her as she walks off. The weight of the air pushed by their wings propels us forward, almost forcing us into a run. The three watch malevolent, but ultimately they are afraid. I hear it in their voices. She does not look back, just drags me forward, and when the lizards turn in the air and fly away, the beat of their wings slowly turns into a silence so profound it fills the plain. I can hold it in my hands. We keep walking, and eventually she lets go of my hand, and I see she is tired but know better than to comfort her.

Neither of us mention the smoke, but soon we can smell it, acrid and menacing. As we get closer to our village, she pauses to pull her long skirt from her slingbag and to pull it on over her leather hunting pants. She takes off her cap and frees her long, red hair. We no longer look like twins, and I know the routine; we will resume our roles: me the older brother, the courageous new lizard reaper, and her— the younger, helpful-but-weak sister. She hands me the lizard's foot. In rigor it has curled and now set. It will stay like that until we cut it up and sell the skin, and talons. We will keep the bones to carve into arrow heads that cannot miss, needles that can pierce even the thickest leather, and sharp daggers that leave flesh rent, impossible to stich, as the wound will rupture. But first we will drain their marrow; it makes the healing salve the villagers all rely on. If we did not provide it, I know they would not tolerate us, the foundlings. The spray of lizard blood across my face and clothes makes me extra convincing this time, and I straighten up and proceed to swagger, but no one runs to meet us. When I look at her, she seems as surprised as I do but shrugs her shoulders. She doesn't get any glory anyway; it's I who feels cheated. Usually everyone comes to cheer and marvel at the lizard claws we bring home. Sometimes they even sing the ballad of the lizard king and put my name in place of the first reaper who slew the terrible ones. I get to swing my sword and reenact the battle and she tells them how brave I was.

Instead of going home and washing the disgusting blood off our skin and clothes, we search out the smoke and walk towards it. I can hear murmurs and crying, and then it stops as we find the whole village gathered, a mute audience watching the last of the flames die out in the ruin of Indri's hut. In front of it, a pole has been thrust into the ground and the telltale flag of the Princeling flaps through the smoke. She looks at me.

"Oswe," she whispers. "We've got to do something."

I don't know what to do or say.

"Oswe," she says again. "Say something!"

I freeze. There is nothing on my tongue because I feel afraid like the rest of them. Only Seren is upright, not bent with the fear of the Princeling and his unnatural alliance with the lizards. She rolls her eyes at me then looks down at the lizard foot. I don't get the hint. She taps it with her finger then mimes waving it in the air. As I am asking her what she means, someone cries out.

"Oswe!! Oswe's back! Oswe will know what to do!"

They brush Seren aside to get to me, marveling at the huge, scaly foot and its frightening talons, assured by my return. In all the years we have been playing these roles, I have never felt so ridiculous or so afraid. If they are relying on me to save them from the Princeling, then we are all doomed. I look to her, but she is behind the villagers, and I can't catch her eye. I can read her face, though; she is trying to figure out a plan. But then something happens that neither of us ever expected; the foot is yanked from my hand, and Indri waves it in my face. It takes both arms and all his strength to wield the heavy foot.

"You! You! The Princeling did this because he thought it was your hut! He came for the lizard reaper!" He spits the words as if I had arranged, somehow, to jeopardize him. He shakes the lizard's claws in my face, and when one scratches my cheek, the crowd gasps as I fall to my knees caterwauling. Seren darts through the crowd and once beside me, crouches and embraces me.

"Get up," she says. "Get up."

She shields me as she looks at the villagers, asking them how they can turn so easily.

"You have relied on Oswe since the old lizard reaper died. What would you do without him?" she demands, her voice strident. "Who would take on the lizards? Who would get you the marrow? Tell me! Tell me!" I've never seen her like this except out on the hunt, and I've never heard say so many words in a row—I am afraid she will give us away.

The villagers shrink back. They were never really our friends, but they look at us as if we haven't lived among them for so many years. They whisper to each other, and I know they are reminding themselves that we appeared on the plain as children, found by the old lizard reaper. They curse him for making the village take us in so he could raise us to care for them when he could no longer do so. We have done this since his death, even though we were too young for such a heavy burden. But the villagers look at us, their eyes hooded and cruel, not unlike the lizards when we are fixed in their stare. Seren pushes my hand, and I get it this time and brandish our sword, the reaping sword. I swirl it in the air, and the sunlight glints from it, the engraving splintering the light into tiny, fiery shards, and they draw back, their misplaced anger transformed into less dangerous mistrust. I walk forward and reclaim the lizard foot from Indri. He cowers from me, staring at the painful wound in my cheek. For just a moment, I know what it feels like to be Seren, to be the real lizard reaper, and then the moment is gone. The foot feels too heavy to carry away, and my arm aches from my sword demonstration. I

217

look over to her. She seems like all the other women now that she has slipped back into her village role, but underneath I sense her dangerous heart, and I know we cannot live here anymore. If she is provoked, it is not just the lizards who will need to hide. Looking at her, it seems so clear now; we were brought here as children, not because we belonged to this tribe but because we didn't. She comes close to me now and takes the foot from my hand.

"We need to leave," she says. "Before it gets worse."

"I know, Seren. They will try to kill us."

She frowns. "No, I mean we will need to leave, so the Princeling doesn't kill them all. He's looking for us, for me. His allegiance is with the terrible ones, and I've hurt so many of them."

"No, he's looking for me, the lizard reaper," I say, and for another brief moment, I feel her strength. "I can turn myself in. The village will be safe, and you can get away."

She shakes her head. "The lizards know the truth, Oswe. He will come to the village again. He will come for me wherever I go."

I know she's right, but I don't know what else to do. My cheek screams. I can feel the laceration from the talon deepening as it continues to tear my flesh. I'm scared now as the wound will eventually splay open. It will seep and fester without the marrow salve.

Seren turns to the crowd. They squint at us nervously. She tells them we are going to our hut to collect our things—then we will leave. They seem to consent until we turn to walk down the alley that will lead us there. Someone calls out that the Princeling will not be satisfied by our departure; they must give us to him. Seren is incensed and she grabs the sword from me and whirls around.

"You idiots!" she screams at them. We are not sneaking away to hide while the Princeling burns you out of your homes and your skins!

The sword, so light in her hand, glints as she plants her feet on the stamped earth and shouts at them with her whole body. Despite her feminine garb, she looks seven feet tall—like a Princeling, not one of the Plainsmen, but I know we are not Princelings. We have talked about this on and off our whole lives. We are not of them, we are not those, but we must come from somewhere and someone. I remember so little except darkness and a soft female voice charging Seren with my care. The lizard reaper told us nothing but taught us the ways of the tribe, and then the hunt. We heard the rumors of other tribes and peoples, and the warning tales told to wilful boys of a tribe where women are the warriors, but no one in the village in this life time has ever seen one. In this life time no one has travelled beyond the edge of the plains; it is not allowed. She continues shouting at them, and I am so busy watching the crowd, wondering when they will rush us and try to kill us now we are denounced, that I don't really hear her words, just the change in her tone—she has stopped berating them; now she commands.

"I have hunted for you. I have protected you. I will go to the Princeling myself."

Feeling her force, the crowd calms and steps back from us. They cannot believe, however, that a woman is their protector. Women's lives are proscribed in this village, and they are written small. They can birth and they can heal, and she has hidden herself in their deference. I am as shocked as them to hear so many words come from her. The villagers turn towards me again and, seeing my gaping wound, it is clear they may have killed me already. I reach up to my cheek knowing it is about to split completely open. One of the healer women, Ardena, comes forward with her jar of marrow salve. It smarts as she shoves it into the wound with her fingers, but it works immediately and I feel the tearing stop. I will live, but I will bear a large, angry scar. The woman who tends me searches my face as she does so. I don't know what she is looking for, but when she is finished, she backs away and talks with her helper. They look over to my sister, scouring her face for something then talking to each other again in whispers.

Now the dangerous tension has gone and the fire has burned itself out, Seren deflates, losing her magnificence and looking like a quiet village girl once again. The villagers talk amongst themselves awkwardly then begin to disperse. I take my my sister's hand and we walk to our hut. No longer hiding her abilities, she rests the flat of her sword's blade on her shoulder and drags the lizard foot home behind her. Its claws score the ground.

When we get to our hut, we find the healer and her assistant have arrived before us. They are seated at our table, looking anxious but intent. My sister ignores them as she rips off her skirt. Both Ardena and her helper gasp as they see Seren's hunting garb beneath, her forbidden trousers.

"You are not a lizard reaper," says the healer. I cough

nervously. Ardena then fixes her gaze on me. "And you, you are definitely not a lizard reaper." I am unused to feeling so small and useless when we are in the village or a woman other than my sister talking to me in this way. She proceeds to ignore me as she tell Serens we are Kala. I spit out my water and look at her. Her brows are knitted.

"If I was Kala, I would have no brother," she says. The healer smiles, and something glimmers in me, a lost knowledge. Something about Seren.

"Maybe that is why you are here."

Seren dismisses them but doesn't say anything more to me. If she is Kala, she won't want me around. I am sure she is thinking through how to abandon me, or worse. I know the stories; no one around here has ever seen the Kala, the women warriors of scare tales. I watch her as she examines her hands and arms, looking closely at her own skin. She calls me over and asks me to look in her eyes, behind her ears, then through her hair. I ask what I am looking for, but she does not know. There is nothing there, no marks or signs; our skins look the same as the rest of the villagers'. We are both taller than most, but not extraordinarily so. I know we were left on the plain, but we never seriously thought it wasn't by other Plainsmen.

While I'm worrying about our origins, Seren has begun to pack essentials. I know better than to ask her about it or to suggest what we should take. Soon she hands me a bag and slings her own over her shoulder, along with the bow and quiver she uses to hunt for food.

"We're leaving," she says. "I don't think we will come back."

As I begin to open the door, she hands me a long, curved dagger, one I carved myself from the talon of a particularly large lizard. It is my best creation yet and was to be sold at the next gathering of the villages, but now I loop its sheath onto my belt and worry that she will expect me to use it. When I do open the door, it seems like the whole village is standing outside blocking the path, and the air is thick with threat. They watch as we come out, parting silently as my sister confidently walks forward towards them. No one says anything until we pass, and when they do, they hiss the word for outsiders.

*Fools. Don't you know she is going to save you?*

Someone spits on the ground behind me, but I follow Seren and say nothing.

When we walk past the last hut of the village, I turn back and see them standing there, straining as if held by a giant hand. They shout at us, and it is clear we are not allowed to return. As we walk out into the plain, each step takes us further from our home and adds incrementally to my fear. It is not the same anxiety of the lizard hunt. As terrifying as that is, I know she will handle it somehow, and I just have to keep out of the way. On hunts I only have to keep my fear under control enough to stop me from running, screaming—like I did the first time we went out with the old reaper. This fear is different; it is cold and makes my limbs heavy. Although she seems to know where we are going, following becomes increasingly difficult. When I drop behind, she walks back and takes my arm, but she does not talk to me. I start to worry that she will abandon me once we are far enough away.

We camp in the open plain, and she stays awake to watch, but I sleep poorly, worrying that she will leave. Finding me awake, she lets me keep watch so she can rest, and my fear abates. I watch the plain and I watch her, and I wonder what marks she thought I would find. We walk for three days, barely talking, just walking and watching, and eventually I see the towers of the castle fort in the distance.

Then I hear the screeching.

I turn and see three lizards flying towards us. I feel the

wind generated by their wings before I hear them beating, but she never turns except to grab my arm and haul me on towards the castle fort. I stumble and she glares, but helps me up then pushes me forward in front of her. The sound of their wings becomes thunder as they are nearly on top of us—their shadows engulf us as they block the sky—but they never slow. Just as quickly they have flown past us, and they continue toward the stone stronghold. I am full of questions, but I know Seren will not answer them, so I stumble on and no more than a minute later an arrow lands at our feet, its point eating into the earth. Attached to it there is a message: *Give us the boy.*

I feel insulted—I am seventeen, almost a man. She looks perplexed then turns fully around and looks at me, her eyes narrowed. Without saying anything, she pulls the arrow out of the ground and adds it to her own quiver. She grabs my arm and we start walking again.

"We could just go the other way," I say. We can go to the mountains.

She doesn't answer me. I know she promised the villagers we would stop the Princeling from going back there, but now that we are exiled I don't understand why we still have to confront him. Why must Seren try to protect them? What I do know is not to ask her. As we continue walking, the stone walls grow bigger and more lizards fly overhead. We see them all landing and perching on the battlements, watching us as we approach. I have never seen anything as big as the castle fort, neither of us has, and my legs grow heavier. If she wasn't dragging me, I would sink to the ground. I can hear the lizards hissing and squealing, and the sounds are so close to words that I swear they are calling us.

"Do you hear them?" I ask, but she looks at me as if I am mad.

They get louder and louder and loom above us, leaning over and cawing at us as we stand at the gate in the wall. Now I can distinctly hear my name in their calls, and then hers, too, and I can't help but notice some of the lizards have one foot smaller and greener than the other. She doesn't even look up at the lizards, but it is clearly an effort; her skin is flushed and her veins stand out, her hand keeps twitching on the hilt of her sword. Before us the gate swings open, and in the courtyard is the largest, oldest lizard we have ever seen. It is so old its green hide has faded to silver. Standing between its claws is the Princeling.

He reaches out his hand to Seren. She does not move, but her eyes are huge. It is as if she is seeing something that I cannot. I look at my feet, but then I hear her speak.

"Do you really want him? Why?"

The Princeling ignores her and looks at me. The ancient lizard opens one eye and looks at me, too. I am caught for a moment in its great emerald and amber gaze, but it lets me go. It hisses and the Princeling tenses.

"You are forgiven," he says to me grudgingly. "You did not know."

His voice scares me. It has an undertone, a sibilance that does not sound quite human. I am scared to look at him, but when I do, I see he holds his sword in his left hand because his right arm ends just below the elbow. It is capped with a silver sheath. I look to my sister for confirmation, but she does not acknowledge me at all, just as the Princeling will not acknowledge her. He catches me looking at his stump and, not letting go of my glance, he rubs the silver cap.

"I will not kill her, if she gives it back."

I have no idea what he is talking about, but she quickly tells me to take out the dagger, and when I do, the lizards all rear back, trumpeting their alarm. The ancient lizard, however, stays perfectly still, except for the flicker of its

inner eyelids which blink twice as it focuses on the blade.
I carved it with the symbols for courage and resolve,
Seren's symbols, and I can see the old one is reading them.
Its tongue flickers from its mouth as it softly hisses at me.
Its words almost reach me. I realize she is female, she is the
oldest one, the queen of lizards. The Princeling is
quivering, barely containing his rage, and I feel the need to
run. Seren puts her hand on my shoulder without even
looking at me.

"Stay still. Stay there."

I stay still, as still as I can. She takes the dagger from me
and places the blade in the flat of her hand as she walks
towards the Princeling. She offers him the hilt, and I'm sure
he is going to take it and slice her fingers off or plunge the
dagger into her.

"This is all that is left. I give it to you."

The princeling gingerly takes the dagger, at once
repelled and admiring. He bends his head to it and rubs his
cheek against the engraved face.

"I did not know. Forgive me."

Then she turns her head away from him in deference and
unwittingly looks straight into the eye of the Queen. Her
whole body freezes, and I know the Queen has caught her

in her ancient gaze and can command her. Suddenly she walks past the Princeling and in between the queen's claws, right up to her head, and she lays her head on her snout just below her huge eye. She is framed in the emerald and amber by the great, whirling knowledge of the oldest of the lizards. I see her reflected there again and again in the depths of the giant eye.

"Seren." I cry out.

The lizard blinks both inner and outer lids, letting my sister go. She stands up and walks to me slowly as the queen begins to hiss again, and this time I hear the words.

"Go home."

She takes my hand and picks up her bag, bidding me to pick up mine, and we walk out. Every lizard's eyes are trained on us, and they twitch from tooth to tail with displeasure but do not dare disobey their ancient queen. We walk in silence and we are not pursued. We walk for days then weeks. We walk so far away that the plains are cut by rivers we swim through, then we reach foothills, and then we must find our way through the mountains I had never really believed in. She tells me the queen lizard spoke to her inside her own mind, but she will not tell me what she said, except the command that I heard, too. Seren is taking me home, but I don't know where that is. Sometimes we see lizards flying in the distance, and sometimes birds I cannot name that never came to the plains. She never tells me where we are going, but she seems to know the way, and when we clear the last mountain pass, we gaze down on valleys and rivers and carpets of trees. I am exhausted and cold and we have both grown skinny and sinewy. When we don't descend but make our rude camp on a craggy outcropping, I begin to lose hope. The future is below us, but she keeps us here. I try not to show my faithlessness, but my despair cannot be contained and I begin to weep.

"We have to wait," she says. Her first words in days, and she falls quiet again.

Her silence fills me with dread. She pats my arm, and later she strokes my hair as I fall asleep. In the morning I realize she is gone, and I look all around. Then I see her standing on another crag looking down into the valley. A column of people is climbing the foothills. They look up at us and gesture and move their mouths; they must be calling to us. I cannot hear them yet, but I see her face is wet with tears. I have never seen them before, and they frighten me. I walk over to her and we stand together waiting for them as they slowly make their way towards us. Eventually I can make out the cries and shouts.

"Oswe, Oswe!"

But no one calls Seren's name. Finally as they draw near, she goes and packs up our few belongings, straightens her hair, and relaces her boots. She still says nothing, but when they appear on the path leading to the crag she calls me to her. In her matter of fact tone, the one she has always used when telling me to clean up after myself, she says, "I am not your sister, Oswe. I am Kala. I was born your protector; the lizard queen told me. There is much to know, but your people will tell you. Now they are here to take you home and I must go and find mine."

"But where?"

"I have to go north," she says as she starts to turn away. "The lizard queen told me, and I must obey."

"But you have to stay with me! You're my sister!" I cry, but before I can follow her, I feel a hand on my shoulder. The woman who will claim to be my mother engulfs me with relief and love and joy as Seren drops all claim to me and walks away. She will not be harmed; they will always be grateful she has kept me safe, but now I must go with the Hidra, from whom I was taken. They cry and hug me one by one, wrapping me in tears and a warmth I have never imagined, but I am chilled by the sibilance of their loving voices. I see Seren in the distance, making her way across the crags, but I lose sight of her as I am surrounded by the Hidra cheering and welcoming their lost prince home. We are forgiven, they tell me, for mutilating our kin. They mean it, they do forgive us; they understand we did not know, there is so much we did not know, but I am brought back now. I am home and all is as it should be. We begin to walk down to the valley, and I am surrounded by jubilant love, but I am alone without my sister.

I have no sister.

Bereft, I weep for Seren; they understand my grief and try to comfort me.

"She is Kala," says my mother, again and again. "She is Kala; she was born to protect you, and she did."

# The Blossom War

*Robert W. Caldwell*

### I. The Incident

Inspire me, O muse; and channel through

my veins, the song of a blossom, plucked

by a graceful paw, and the gruesome war

that followed, in which hundreds of souls

descended, too soon, into the Undergloom—

Minuend's dismal realm of drifting souls.

I sing of Shineclaw Palace, and the elder

Shineclaw himself, a noble, who ruled

Talea, and green-eyed Grizelda

his daughter so beautiful. I sing too

of the noble saur Clomprock, who strolls

down a path and whistles. His pet boclar

running and jumping. Happy he is,

as well he should be.

Our hero stops

at the wooden gate, and pulls the bell rope,

while his pet, Dccno, chascs a bird.

A servant lean, with sunken eyes, greets him.

Our hero follows the aged saur through the

233

door

and down a long, decorated hall
of rare wood. When they reach a banquet room
the servant departs, leaving Clomprock to sit
on a stone chair by a granite-top table
with silver candlesticks. A crystal
chandelier gleamed from above, with a warm glow.

Old Shineclaw with his daughter enters,

The old saur sits down in a chair, then lifts
his mug and enjoins, "This is a great day!
You two become one; so also our kingdoms
unite."

Grizelda's big green eyes gaze
at Clomprock; her smile is stunning, her tail
exquisite, her scales rainbow hued and shiny.

Sheilida, the comely goddess of love
sits unseen in a corner smiling
upon the two lovers, and sighing.

After dinner Grizelda and Clomprock
stroll through the Shineclaw garden.

Grizelda

says,
"These baldons are the prettiest of all.

234

I tell the gardener to water and prune
them each day."

Sheilida uses just a bit
of her power to enhance the pull
between the betrothed pair. Grizelda
pauses at a patch of purple flowers,
"…and these are my special favorites!"

Clomprock picks a delicate bloom and says,
"This evening won't end 'til this blossom fades."

Grizelda's green eyes turn a fiery red.
The slitted pupils blaze as she growls,
"What have you done!"

Clomprock asks, "What's
wrong?"

Grizelda, sharp teeth gleaming, cries out.
"How dare you disturb my logirams!"

Bapoo
the butler, approaches with six guards in tow.
"What is going on?" Bapoo stands erect
with a bearing of self-importance.
"I merely picked a blossom," Clomprock says.
Grizelda glares at him, her green eyes now
stones. In a low growl she says, "That's a lie."

Sheilida looks on in horror, gasping.

Knowing that no one would find picking

A flower to be as horrible

As she knows it to be, Grizelda

Decides to say something quite ugly.

"He tried to kiss me, and do more than that."

Bapoo orders his saurs to seize Clomprock,

They surround him and grab hold of him.

Fighting to escape their hold, Clomprock ask,

"What are you doing?"

Aged Shineclaw ambles

over and asks gently, "What has happened?"

Before his accusers can interrupt,

Clomprock seizes the chance to answer the charge.

"I picked this bloom as a token of love."

A shadow smile spreads across Shineclaw's

face.

Sheilida, the pretty goddess, franticly

waves her arms to send energy into

Grizelda, but the angry girl remains

unmoved. "Liar!" She bursts, "He assaulted me!"

The six assailants push Clomprock toward the

house;

but the brawny male has other ideas.

He forces himself free and jumps the fence.

Bapoo, and the loyal servants, chase after.

In the scuffle, the flower falls to the ground.

Sheilida, the gorgeous one, in panic

flees to her bedroom and falls face down

where she writhes and sobs in agony.

Her husband, Torv, the leader of gods,

crawls into bed with her, snuggles up

against the fair goddess and comforts her.

Grizelda, left with her puzzled father,

picks up the insulting bloom and ponders

the fragment of beauty so shamelessly plucked.

Clomprock barely outpaces the pursuit.

One creature comes to his aid, Deeno.

The boclar snaps his jaws, and jumps on Bapoo.

Deeno's sharp talons scratch the butler's face,

almost gouging out one of his eyes.

This diversion gives Clomprock time enough

to assume a fighting posture and slash

his sinewy tail against the onrushing

servants.

But more attackers appear. Clomprock,

with only his boclar to help, fights them off
and steps backward toward the path then dashes off.
Deeno, with one final hiss, follows.
They run through fields and woods, covering vast
distances with ease. All night Clomprock runs;
he is his own steed. Back to his kingdom
he sprints, back to his friends, and his palace.

## II. Gathering of Allies

Word spreads faster than Clomprock can
run.
He has just wiped the dust from his feet when
Litnet, the constable, rings the bell at
Clomprock's gate. "Come along now, peaceful."

"Why?" shouts Clomprock from inside his
house.

"You know why," replies Litnet, "Must I
use force?"

"What do you know, other than what you
heard?
by law, I am entitled to a trial."

"Your crime was despicable, you must
come…"
A loud yelp is heard from behind the house.

"Your troops tried to sneak in the back
way,"
says Clomprock. "They didn't reckon on
my trusted boclar, Deeno. Now please leave."
At that, Clomprock's loyal servants toss
pebbles at the rotund constable who
stumbles as he ambles away.

Some saurs there are, loyal but few, who

gather

around the standard of Clomprock. They

are ones, who, despite distorted rumors

casting blame on him, disbelieve the tales,

such is their faith in the saur. Important

among these are Clapper and his five sons.

Lionfeld, ruler of the small kingdom

of Ganser, who commands a small army,

Galladont, ruler of the third largest

kingdom in the land, who leads a large force

of well trained rock-hurlers; and Ajathrax

whose archers are second to none. They work to

strengthen the defenses around Clomprock's house,

stacking stones, sharpening poles.

However

the greater majority sympathize

with Shineclaw and flock to bolster the

avenging force to the point where it looks

as though the cause is won by numbers alone.

The first to run to Shineclaw's aid is

Barxdale,

a rival suitor for Grizelda's hand.

He brings a frightening troop of trained rupters.

Bapoo greets him, "A change in fortune

has brought Grizelda back to you. Wait here."
Grizelda flicks her tongue as she enters
the room.

Flying down from her bedroom, Sheilida
beckons with all her energy to persuade
Grizelda to reconsider, but a flame
that Sheilida herself planted
in Grizelda's heart, still burns for Barxdale.

Shineclaw exclaims, "What's that lad
doing here?"
Grizelda and Barxdale vanish into
a bedroom. Shineclaw feebly shouts, "Barxdale
was banished! What's going on here? Grrrr.
And who are all these saurs gathered outside
demanding to see me?"

Bapoo doesn't
reply, but places his body in the
doorway, blocking Shineclaw's exit. Astounded
Shineclaw stares at Bapoo. "Why are you holding
me prisoner in my own house?" Servants
grab him, and tie him with rope.

Bapoo sneers,
"For years I have waited for this moment."

"But why? Bapoo, my loyal servant, why?"

Shouts feeble Shineclaw as he is dragged off.

Shining Sheilida, oblivious
to what passed  between Bapoo and Shineclaw
weeps. Her husband walks up behind her
and takes her into his arms.

"What kind of
goddess am I if my powers are so
useless?" She weeps on his shoulder.

"There now
fairest among females," says Torv. "Love
has a will of its own. You can only
influence love the way you can tame a river."

Others unsavory who allied with
Shineclaw, (unwilling puppet of Bapoo)
are Litnet, the chief constable (who
we already met) and his bumbling cops;
Magosaur, who commands a large army;
Nilihum, and his squad of champion
rock-hurlers; but the most despicable
of all is Slimenerd.

Bapoo addresses
the assembled leaders, "My friends!" he shouts,
"To avenge this grievous wrong, we should not
be gathered here! Our place is in the fight!

Let us march to Clomprock's castle and lay siege."

"Who are you?" shouts Claptrap, "Where is Shineclaw?"

"He is ill," replies smooth talking Bapoo.

"Shineclaw has always been a hearty saur," says Claptrap, "and I don't remember him appointing *you* his spokesman."

"Bring out Shineclaw!"
Some creatures in the crowd shout.

But replies Bapoo, "I told you, he is gravely ill!"

"There is something strange going on here," says
Claptrap. "I will not support you unless I talk to Shineclaw in person."

"You can see him when he gets better," says Bapoo as Claptrap turns and leaves the gathering. He is followed by many others who begin to march. They travel at a fast pace along the cobblestone road they sprint. For a day and a night they run without wearying, to Clomprock's kingdom they travel and receive a warm welcome at his gate.

Meanwhile, smooth talking Bapoo rallies the troops.

"Begin the march!" He shouts, "We shall gather at the crossroads. I'll meet you there" He exits.

Inside Bapoo conspires with Slimenerd.
"Are you
with me?"

Replies Slimenerd, "What do I get out of it?"

"Why Grizelda of course!"

Slimenerd bares his fangs, his grin evil.
"Yesss!"

Bapoo calls Grizelda who breaks away from Barxdale and enters the rooms. "Yes Bapoo, what do you want?"

"It is my pleasure
to introduce you to Slimenerd."

She shakes,
"But we've already met." Bapoo slithers out and slams the door, trapping her in the room. Slimenerd approaches, and jumps, forcing her to the floor. Grizelda screams and struggles.

Sheilida can only look on in horror.

A different force is at work here than love.

Barxdale runs down the hall and sees Bapoo
standing in front of the door.

"What's he doing
to Grizelda?" He shouts over the sounds
of screaming and thumping. Bapoo turns and
glares at him with bared fangs and replies.

"Nothing. Do you understand? Nothing."
Sheilida shoots her magic at him
to try to arouse a gallant sprit
that will compel him to rescue her.
But his love proves to be only shallow.
Barxdale slowly backs away and retreats.

Bapoo appoints a guard to stand by the door
and then walks to the crossroads and takes
his place at the front of the column.
"Onward, let's defeat that scoundrel Clomprock!"
A cheer wells up when Bapoo takes a step
The first step of the march. All that day
and the next, Bapoo's army marches.
Along the cobblestone road, they sprint.
For a day and a night they run without
weariness. To Clomprock's kingdom they travel.

### III. The Talisman

Ashteron, the god of disorder, awakes

when Chaos charges into the room

shouting, "Something has happened which you'll

like!"

Angered by the intrusion, Ashteron

tosses Chaos against the wall and tries to

go back to sleep. But Chaos pulls herself

off the floor and shouts, "It's a war! A war

has broken out!" Then she runs away

before wrathful Ashteron can throw her

again. When he is ready to get up,

the evil god Ashteron leaves his bed

and watches the events of the last two days

as if they were presently happening.

Then he calls Chaos. As she cowers

before him, the evil god says, "Go fetch

me the flower that Clomprock picked!" Chaos flies

away descending from the ethereal

realm to the time and place where the flower fell.

Then, unseen by mortals, she sails upward

returning to the ethereal realm

and hands the flower to Ashteron who

rewards her with a blow to the head.

Ashteron takes the flower to the furnace
where Nacluv, the god of hard work, sweats
at his forge. Barging in, Ashteron shouts,
"Nacluv! Stop your work and do my task now."

"Yes, sir." The brawny god's hammer
clangs
to a stop. Shadowy Ashteron groans,
"I want this flower plated in gold."

"But sir," pleads Nacluv shaking. "That will
be…"

"No 'But sirs!' booms Ashteron striking
Nacluv,
"Just do it!" Trembling, the sweat god discerns
how he can do the impossible.
He places the flower in a cauldron
which contains a solution of liquid gold.
The flower begins to fossilize.

"This will take a while," murmurs Nacluv,
bracing
himself for a blow.

"Bring it to me when
you're finished." The Evil god departs,
and Nacluv breathes a sigh of relief.

A few months later, Nacluv removes the

golden blossom from the brew. To it he
adds diamonds to replace the stamen,
and coats the stem with silver. Reluctantly
he carries the finished piece to Ashteron
who snatches it from his paw without so
much as a thank you.

The evil god pours
some magic onto the golden bloom then
descends to the land and zips backward in
time to where the battle rages before
Clomprock's once humble abode. He places
the gilded flower into Bapoo's hand.

Bapoo discovers the blossom as he
prepares to enter the fray and
is elated by this sign from the gods
which he places on his staff.

Magosaur walks with Bapoo toward the
house
his slingshot corps gets ready to fire.
They pull back the pouches, take aim, and unleash
a volley. Some of the soldiers on the wall
fall dead, but Ajathrax, and his squad
of archers shoot back and many more
of the enemy fall. Those that can

master the bow are rare, and Ajathrax
and his corps are the best. But Nilihum
and his rock-hurlers fling rocks upon the wall
and reek havoc among Clomprock's saurs.

      Gallodont orders his troops to hurl away.
His champions, with the advantage
of their high spot on the wall, decimate
Nihilum's troops, and cause great havoc.
Bapoo raises his staff and calls his saurs
to action. Along his entire line
spears sail, rocks fly. He pushes his greater
numbers against the wall expecting
inevitable collapse.

      Behind
the fray, Barxdale tends to his rupters.
Unable to take part in the battle
the creatures snarl and pull at their tethers.
Barxdale holds out clumps of meat
and expertly whisks his paws away
as they snap. "Be patient my darlings,"
he says gently. "When those walls come down
you'll have your chance." From the nearby tent
he hears moans. Slimenerd has his way with
Grizelda.

"I like it when you do that,"
Slimenerd hisses. Barxdale trembles in rage.
He longs to rush in and rescue her,
but he can't. He just doesn't have the nerve
to face him. "I am *his* rupter," Barxdale sighs.

Meanwhile in the midst of the fighting
a fresh youth approaches Clomprock unfazed
by the projectiles flying through the air.
"Clomprock, I will tell you a secret.
You are one of my chosen ones for the
battle at the end of time, but right now
you are destined for a different task.
Follow me, and you shall obtain the

Talisman." The fresh youth is none other
than
Torv, the creator. "You need not worry
about the battle while you're gone. I'll cast
a happy spell over the enemy
so that their hearts will not be in the fight."

He transforms into a bird with rainbow
plumage and invites Clomprock to hop
onto his back. Off into the sky they soar.
In only a little time they arrive
at the entrance to Minuend's domain.

Here the fiery Talisman is kept guarded,

a magical weapon that can only

be obtained by the pure of heart.

                                             Torv

transforms back into a youth and then follows

Clomprock into the cave, they descend

into the grim Undergloom. After

many hours of walking, they reach

a huge cavern. An iron gate bars entry,

and a long line of souls waits for admittance.

Torv drags Clomprock to the front of the line,

but the gaunt Keeper grasps Torv by the tail.

       "Living souls cannot enter without a…"

       "We'll see about that!" Clomprock tackles

the Keeper and wrestles with the spirit.

The Keeper is surprisingly strong,

but so is Clomprock, who immediately

gains the upper hand. Slowly though, the Keeper

prevails, and locks Clomprock into a hold.

"Very good Clomprock!" says Torv. "That's

enough.

You'll need your strength later."

                                     Torv starts to pass

through the gate, but the Keeper stops him shouting,

"Wait! Living souls must fill out a visitors form!"

"I don't need to fill out anything," says
Torv. "I created you! And everything
here. And Clomprock, though not dead, is allowed
to enter without filling out a form."

"Well, ah, I didn't know! You see, ah, you
don't look like a god."

"Hey, don't sweat," says
Torv
as he and Clomprock pass through the gate.
They enter a wide plain filled with creatures
engaged in a range of activities.

Torv says, "These are creatures who created
stupid inventions. They are forced, for a
time to have to use them. Clomprock sees a
saur pull the drawstring of a slingshot.
One of the ends comes loose and slaps his face.
Another saur tries to drive a stake into
the ground with a sledge hammer, but the head
keeps falling off onto his foot. He sees
a female whose exhausted tail lays sprawled,
a heavy ornament tied to it.

"Here we enter the land where unkind souls
are tortured by their own voices blaring

what they told others during life. Try not
to listen."

Clomprock hears a gravelly voiced,
"Ugly!"
Then a smooth, "I only want to be your friend."
They trudge a long way over mushy ground.
The polished words, "I promise." "If you loved
me…"
and the like, make the walking more tedious.
Clomprock is glad to hear, "This is the land
of petty crimes," though he is afraid
of what awaits them there. He wonders
how much farther they have yet to go.

Minuend himself appears, and thunders,
"What are you doing here?"

Torv calmly
answers, "The champion Clomprock has come
to take the Talisman."

"The poor fool
will end up like the others!" The god
of the Undergloom points toward a far field
where twisted saurs hang from crosses. He mutters,
"What a waste."

"No, Clomprock is the destined

one."

Minuend bares his fangs in a vile grin,
"I think I'll stick around and watch him try.
It might actually be entertaining."
The field of crosses gets closer. Clomprock
glances to the right, passed the petty crime
sufferers (a saur bound, legs and arms
stretched out while a steady drip of water
falls on his face, a female who has
a piece of flesh constantly bitten off her
and replaced) toward a large, domed building.

"That is your destiny Clomprock," says
Torv.
"The place where I gather my champions
for the final battle against evil."

"Not if he fails to fetch the Talisman,"
mutters the god of the Undergloom.

The field is now closer,
behind it is a much larger domed building.

"That is where Ashteron gathers his group
of champions," Torv says. Clomprock gulps.
and at that moment he beholds the flaming
torch nestled in a stone pedestal.
Clomprock pauses, then takes off in a sprint.

Fire springs forth flowing over the ground
engulfing Clomprock, but he is unafraid
and thus unharmed. "He passed the first test,"
says Minuend, as Clomprock reaches
for the handle with his three-toed hand.
Vines sprout, which quickly cover the Talisman
and wrap around him, Clomprock begins
to choke, he struggles, but the vines grip
only tightens. Clomprock claws furiously
at the vines, but no sooner does he rip
them away than they grow back squeezing harder.
With pure determination he clears them
away in time to grasp the handle.
Instantly the vines vanish.

                       "Second test."
says Minuend. Clomprock pulls with all his might
and slowly withdraws the Talisman from
the pedestal. As he lifts it aloft
and turns to face Torv, grinning, the creatures
on the crosses are released. They gather
around Clomprock. Some are tall, some are small.
One is the legendary Odop
warrior female of many a bard's tale.
Others are extinct species; a stegon.

an iguan, a sauropod.

"These worthy
contenders are your servants," says Torv.

Minuend adds, "Third Test!" as Torv,
Clomprock,
and the army of heroes march out
of the Undergloom. "We'd better hurry,"
says Torv, "My calming spell weakens."

## IV. Turning of the Tide

Litnet paces impatiently along

the line of siege. "What's wrong with you saurs?"

he shouts,

"Smiling like idiots, you have hardly

cast a spear or thrown a rock all afternoon!

Some constables you are. First you let

Clomprock walk away, now you fight sluggishly.

Ashteron enhances his temper

with a spell, working Litnet into

an even greater rage, prompting him

to walk away from the line, closer

to Clomprock's house. He issues a challenge.

"Come out you warriors and fight like saurs.

Quit cowering behind those weak walls!

Face your just desserts, followers of

the female-hitter."

Clapper shoots his reply.

Litnet dodges the shot and returns

one of his own which strikes Clapper's torso

and knocks him over. Clapper's eldest son

jumps off the wall and charges Litnet.

"Get back Urn! Don't be foolish," Clapper

shouts.

"You shall pay for striking my father!" Urn
calls.
He shoots a nice hard rock which strikes Litnet
in the face. The constable, instead
of shooting back, charges Urn, and pounces.
He lands on top of him with slashing claws
and rips a huge gash down Urn's side.

Clapper jumps off the wall and charges.
He lashes Litnet with the whip that is
attached to the tip of his tail then slashes
the constable, disemboweling him.
Before he can drag his son to safety
one of the remaining constables
eyes Urn's slingshot, and lunges for it.

"That satchel is well made!" says another
and joins the charge. Clapper whips the two.
Ajathrax's archers launch a barrage
of arrows which fell the looting pair.
Clapper drags his injured son away.
The remaining constables eye Litnet's
slingshot, and his hat. They move out to plunder.
No one on Clomprock's side contests them.
The two tussle over the slingshot then
throw dice to see who gets the hat. Then their

mouths water over the nice fat body—
choice meat that no carnivore can ignore.

      Bapoo walks along the line, scowling.
Nowhere else is there any fighting.
"What's the matter with you guys?" he growls.
"We didn't march so many hundred leagues
just to stand around grinning like idiots."
He waves the gilded blossom and energy
flows into the troops, renewed spirit fills them.
Magosaur orders his saurs to shoot.
Nilihum orders his remnant rock-hurlers
to throw. Those in the beleaguered fort
fight back and the battle begins to rage.

      Bapoo spies Barxdale standing beside
his rupters, and screams, "Don't stand there
dawdling,"

      "But I have to watch the..." Barxdale utters.

      Bapoo growls and slashes with his tail whip,
"Get in the fight!" The diminutive saur
stumbles forward, unsure what to do.

      Catapults fire. Boulders strike the walls.
One smashes Claptrap. A fleeting image
of his mate and offspring flashes in his mind.
Where he had stood the masonry crumbles,

creating a breach in the castle wall.

Bapoo barges into Slimenerd's tent,
"Stop sexing your female. Come out and fight!"
Slimenerd turns and snarls, "How dare you enter
my private tent!"

"I am the commander,
I can enter any tent I want!"
Bapoo waves the gilded blossom at the lean,
nondescript saur.

"Don't wave your little charm
at me," Slimenerd rolls off the bed and slashes
Bapoo.

"Are you going to fight, or are you
going to play with your little toy?"
Bapoo whips the prone form, which lays on the bed
with glazed green eyes. Grizelda doesn't even
jump. Slimenerd grabs Bapoo and digs his claws
into his flesh with surprising strength.
Bapoo throws him and growls, "Get out there!"
then whips him once for good measure before
he turns and leaves. Slimenerd mutters, "I'll kill
him.
He thinks he's the one in charge here."

Barxdale sneaks back to his trained rupters

and, using his sharp claws, cuts the tether.

They run toward the breach, ready to invade.

Something slightly larger than them streaks out.

It is Deeno. The boclar takes out

six rupters without even getting a scratch.

The rest of the pack, though, heads into the breach.

But a rivulet of fire blocks them.

More streams flow in and engulf soldiers.

Those of the enemy yell and scream

as they are burned alive, except a few

who it spares. They walk away unscathed,

saurs who had been forced to fight for the dark.

Those of Clomprock's troops who feel the flame

experience healing sensations.

One stream climbs the wall and enters the room

where Urn lays. Soothing flames heal his wound.

   The fighting ceases as all look southward,

the direction the path of flame leads.

Through a cloud of dust they see Clomprock

walking and holding a torch aloft.

He leads an army of odd creatures,

some are tall, others are small. Some extinct;

a stegon, an iguan, a sauropod.

Vanished heros of the past march with him.

261

One is Odop, female warrior of legend.

All realize that he holds the Talisman.

Some tremble in dread, others feel great joy.

A cheer rises from Clomprock's ramparts

while Bapoo's army grows silent.

Clomprock marches through the gate into
his house.

He places the fiery Talisman

upon the ramparts. A stream of flame

forms a moat about his fortress, both

a welcome to friends and a warning to foes.

### V. The Persistent Evil

The Talisman lights up the night sky.

Dancing flames encircle Clomprock's domain.

Inside, he rests secure, believing

the battle to be over and won,

for no enemy would attack an army

which has this gleaming proclamation

declaring the rightness of its cause.

In that belief, he is mistaken.

Nilihum, with his remaining rock-hurlers,

tries to sneak away, but Bapoo catches him.

"Where do you think you're going?" Bapoo growls.

"The Talisman. We can't fight the

Talisman."

Bapoo waves the gilded Blossom in his face.

"Clomprock got it through trickery," he feels

power growing with him. "He can't win.

Its essence will only work against him."

"He can't win," repeats Nilihum, eyes

glazed.

Bapoo waves the gilded blossom at the

troops.

"Clomprock got it through trickery. He can't win.

The Talisman will work against him."

"Work against him," the troops recite.

Slimenerd pounces on Magosaur, "Stop!"
He pins him, "You're not going anywhere."
"But the Talisman! He's got the Talisman."
"I can handle that Talisman easy
I'll give it a good dousing in water.
Now get back!" Slimenerd hits him with a club
then wields it against his troops cowing them
back into the camp. He then searches
for Bapoo. One of the hypnotized
informs him. "Bapoo has gone off to seek allies."
"Allies? Who?"
"Big Heads."
"Is he
crazy?"
Meanwhile Bapoo sprints through the
dismal night,
stumbling toward the land of the Big Heads.
He comes upon the slumbering giants
and begins to wave the gilded blossom.
"Come along with me. I have a task
for you to do, a task, a pleasant task,
just a little task." A big eyelid opens

revealing a huge eye which stares at him.

"Come along with me." The Big Head rumbles

and the eye turns red. "I have a task."

The head moves. "A task, a pleasant task."

The creature stirs. "Just a little task."

The Big Head rises until it towers

above Bapoo. Two enormous red eyes

look through him. Undaunted, Bapoo continues.

"Come along with me. I have a task."

The earth thunders, "Who disturbs my

sleep?"

Bapoo waves the gilded blossom, "A task,

a pleasant task, just a little task."

The eyes turn aqua. The tail undulates.

A second Big Head stirs. A mountain rises

and the earth trembles. A second pair

of huge eyes penetrates Bapoo. He sings

"Come along with me. I have a task for you

to do, a task, a pleasant task, just a

little task." He jumps in time to avoid

massive jaws. Without missing a beat

he sings "Come along with me." Those eyes turn

green,

but the first creature's eyes turn slightly red,

and it growls. Bapoo sings to it. "A task.
I have a task for you to do." The earth
trembles and more towers rise. A dozen
red saucers glare at him. Deftly, Bapoo
dodges swinging tails, and snapping jaws,
as he sings to each creature. Somehow
he manages to hypnotize six Big Heads
and lead them off  as he keeps the others dazed.

   Bapoo's task would not have been possible
without divine intervention Ashteron,
watching from the shadows, tells Chaos .
to go help him, and sends the little goddess
off with a kick. She runs around like a mouse
distracting Big Heads that would pursue Bapoo.
Ashteron, cast a spell that makes six more
Big Heads wander off to do Bapoo's bidding.
As the sun Rises Bapoo coaxes
his herd of Big Heads toward Clomprock's castle.

## VI. The End of the Matter

Clomprock and Odop the warrior female

sit in front of a fire. A fire

lighted by the Talisman. Deeno sleeps

at their feet. Odop strokes the boclar.

"The vines, they stop me. I walk right through fire.

But vines. They keep growing. I pull. I pull.

'till I tire. For hours it seems, I pull.

Vines, they finally wrap around me and squeeze

me to death."

Invisible to them,

Sheilida, the goddess of love, watches.

The sultry goddess still pouts over the failed

coupling of Clomprock and Grizelda.

"I admire you for trying to take

The Talisman. You have no reason

to be ashamed." He leans against her.

Inspiration strikes comely Sheilida.

She tosses a pebble at Clomprock

which bounces off his shoulder. He stirs

and observes Odop in a whole new way.

Deeno lifts his head and looks around.

Odop's golden voice purrs, "I on cross many

lifetimes. If I live a thousand years

it not be as long as I hang on cross
suffering great pain. Talisman not worth it."

As he listens, Clomprock becomes intrigued.
This female is a slightly different species,
now extinct. She is smaller, with bony
plates on her skin that form a natural armor.
But this only makes her more exotic.

Sheilida tosses a stone at Odop.
which bounces off the top of her head,
and then hits Deeno who growls softly.

With a start, Odop realizes that
Clomprock is muscular, with big eyes
and dull scales, many of which are broken.
All the more attractive, because of the
hardship he has suffered. The two gaze
into each other's eyes. Deeno lowers
his head, wags his tail, and goes back to sleep.


Barxdale tending his few remaining
rupters watches the sun rise. Slimenerd comes
to him with a hose, and tells him to grab hold.
The army, towing hoses, advances.

"You're kidding, right?" asks Barxdale.

For

reply
Slimenerd kicks him, making sure to swing
his switchblade claw which cuts a gash across
Barxdale's chest.

        "Insolent fool!" exclaims
Slimenerd while he grabs a rupter chain
and squeezes the collar around Barxdale's neck.
He then takes hold of the chain and pulls
him and the rupters, Barxdale lays on
the ground refusing to move. Slimenerd kicks
him again. Reluctantly, Barxdale gets up.

        But nobody is a better expert
on rupter collars than Barxdale. He
releases his lock and the locks of the
rupters, whom he signals to attack.
The creatures fall on Slimenerd, who kicks one
which yelps as it stumbles. The other rupters
head for easier targets taking out
a dozen hose-carrying warriors
before they can be slain. Barxdale turns and
stumbles toward the wall of flame, falls into it
and instantly vaporizes: no trace left.

        Clomprock walks onto the battlements,
Odop at his side and asks "What is

going on?" Slimenerd curses him and

unleashes the water from the hoses.

Just then Big Heads appear, herded by Bapoo.

The water only feeds the flames. Those at

the end of the hoses get swept by fire,

the rest back away. The Big Heads hesitate

as Bapoo urges them forward. Soldiers

on the battlements shoot stones which bounce

off their heads, they shake themselves, look around,

then tear into Bapoo's troops. The Big Heads

clap their jaws to grab the soldiers

then tilt their heads to swallow.

      Upon seeing this, Bapoo's soldiers scatter.

Slimenerd runs up to Bapoo and shouts,

      "You idiot!" then slashes him across

his belly so that the guts spill out.

He grabs the gilded blossom and waves

it in the faces of the nearest saurs.

and orders them, "Run to that distant

clump of trees," he then goes after more troops.

      Slimenerd's task would have been hopeless,

he might

have rallied only a few more saurs,

but for action taken by Ashteron

watching from the shadows. The evil god,

frustrated with Chaos, kicks her aside,

and runs after fleeing soldiers himself

in the guise of Slimenerd. He uses his power

to grip their minds and force them toward the trees.

       The real Slimenerd, finding his escape

cut off, is forced to make a break for safety.

And he would not have made it, engulfing

flames from the Talisman race toward him,

had Ashteron not given him a push

with a power surge that sends him soaring

toward the cluster of trees where the remnant

of his army gathers. He finds

more soldiers there than he expected

for most, upon seeing saurs gathered,

had run in that direction, with some help

from Ashteron. He waves the gilded bloom

and orders the soldiers into woods.

Clomprock pursues leisurely because

 the flames of the Talisman outrace his

troops, mopping up and cleansing, the scattered

soldiers of Slimenerd. Only a few

yell and scream as they are burned alive,

the rest emerge healthier looking

with smiles. They turn and begin to walk home.

Slimenerd spirits away desperate to find

new allies. Looking about he spies

Vegetable Eaters grazing.in a glen

that is next to a forest and runs to

a herd of flat bills. Waving the bloom

he says, "Follow me!"

The flat bills turn

their heads to look at him with one eye

and ask, in a chorus, "Why should we care?"

Slimnerd continues to wave the Blossom

"Follow me, I have work for you to do."

One flat bill says, "Why should I care?" Another

Flat bill says, "I think we'd better leave now."

The herd instantly scatters. Before

Slimenerd can figure out why, he gets grabbed

By sharp teeth, jerked off the ground, and swallowed.

The Big Head catches the gilded blossom

with her short arm as she eats Slimenerd.

Clomprock marches up to the Big Head.

"He bad, I get indigestion," she says

"Here is magic trinket. It belong

to you now." Standing on one leg, the Big Head

takes the flower out of her two toed hand

with her grasping foot and, gives it to Clomprock.

Disgusted, he flings it into the sky.

Helped along by Zing, the messenger god,

the sparkling blossom flies into the sky,

and takes a place among the stars—

where you can see to this very day.

The Big Head slowly wanders away.

Clomrock stumbles into the tent where

Grizelda lies staring into nowhere.

He looks over the lean body with

shattered scales, now with a haunting allure,

but feels love no more, only pity.

"She got punished for her pride far worse

than she deserved. Her scheming led to this."

Odop following behind spies the poor girl

and adjusting a blanket, talks to her

soothingly, and strokes her gently.

Grizelda who stares into nowhere.

Grizelda who walks when told to walk,

but she must be guided, her arm held.

The girl who eats when told to eat, but tastes nothing.

The next day, they prepare to travel

Clomprock places Grizelda on the back

of the sauropod, Billoppo, one of

the heroes he rescued from the crosses

at the Talisman. The creature, now

one of a kind, with sad eyes, laments.

"I thought I'd gotten it and gone home."

He says, "Only to wake up and find myself

on the cross. A thousand times I went home

welcomed as a hero. Living my life.

But waking up again, still on the cross.

I feel that even now, all is but a dream

And I will wake up once more, still on that cross."

The other odd creatures who he rescued,

having nothing else to do, travel along.

some are tall, others are small. Some extinct;

a stegon, an iguan, Vanished heroes

from the past march along with Clomprock.

They pass through fields and woods, to Shineclaw Palace

where he finds the saur dazed, incoherent,

gaunt and wrinkled, aged before his time.

Shineclaw barely speaks and just sits and stares

Clomprock appoints the extinct hero saurs

to be regents, ruling the kingdom.

Shineclaw and Clomprock's kingdoms are united

but not in the way that had been planned.

For aged Shineclaw's lands are now merely

a shadow kingdom ruled by extinct creatures.

"Everything is just a dream, then we wake up

in the Undergloom," says Billoppo.

But Clomprock and Odop think happy thoughts.

They settle in Clomprock's castle, lay eggs

And ranch herds of triple horns. While the rest

of the heroes prepare to go on

a journey, to ride the dragon of Nerf

and return to the lands from which they came.

# The Dying Dragon

*Jim Lee*

Yorub of Oyon climbed the last brush-covered hillock and
paused atop a stone outcropping. Below her the beach
sands glimmered in the faint light. Only a single Guardian
Moon had ventured forth this night—and that was Vesa, the
smallest and weakest of the Most Holy Trio.

She turned her head, eyed the lopsided crescent shape
directly and wondered if it was lonely in the absence of its
siblings.

Did the Denizens of Heaven even have emotions,
fears—or improper desires?

"Nonsense," she told herself, even as she brought the
Talisman to her lips.

Yorub stared out along the Great Green Sea toward
Infinity as she kissed the unpolished, vaguely dragon-
shaped chunk of alder wood. This time, even the familiar
taste and texture of the Sacred Charm could not soothe her.

She released the Talisman and it thumped down between
her breasts. Its modest weight again stretched the leather
strap that had now been about the Dragon Sister's slender
neck for three years without interruption—since the day

that Yorub had taken the Final Oath, in fact.

Now she shivered, despite a sea breeze. Yorub sighed, slowly shook her freshly shaved head. She regarded the deceptive calm.

She considered her weakness—and the accident.

That moderate disaster might easily have been much worse.

*My fault. My responsibility.*

The Way was not easy—but it was hers now. She had willingly, proudly taken the Oath. Now she must simply live by it.

*Simply*!

Yorub snorted.

The encounter itself had been bad enough, the temptation to go farther awful. But her reaction to it—to him—that had been worse than the transgression itself!

That had been childish, self-indulgent—even cowardly.

Ultimately, it proved dangerous to the very people she was sworn to safeguard.

Her coarse nightshirt billowed in the salt breeze. Would she ever see herself a Proper Sister again? And had she ever been one at all, what with such feelings?

She kicked a pebble down onto the deserted beach and struggled with a cloudy memory. She pictured her new superior, Bemba of Ifler's Ridge—an old woman, dimly recalled from her days at the Academy. Slow-moving and slow-speaking, even then; bent almost double by the years, yet stubborn. Yorub wondered if Bemba still took a daily stroll (or hobble, to be both cruel and accurate) among the Citadel's lush outer gardens.

She had taken no courses under her. But it was said Bemba was a stern, demanding instructor—and an arch conservative, though fair.

Would mere fairness be enough?

Again, Yorub shuddered.

Nine days remained before the annual Tour of Inspection was scheduled to reach this outlying village.

*I must confess. Tell of my unfitness, my shameful desires—and of the consequences.*

It was the only way the young Sister might begin to cleanse herself.

But meanwhile, a different problem vexed her. A strange aching feeling she could not name pulled her from a sleepless bed. The emotion, the turmoil was not entirely her own: The Sacred Link was unmistakable and she waited, fear wriggling deep in her gut.

She thrust a defiant jaw out at the darkness. But it was a sham. She knew it well and that meant that the powerful being on the other end would also know.

She was a Priestess, a warrior—and more, a Dragon Sister! Such a leader who could afford no distractions, no complications—even here, along the eastern coast and but one day's ride from the Sacred Alder Woods!

Yorub had allowed herself to forget that basic truth.

Besides, she was now consecrated, committed to a different and higher state of being. The normal weaknesses and failings had no place in her heart.

And yet, there she stood—trembling, afraid.

"Couldn't sleep?" The calm, even tone of his voice made Yorub gasp. "Me neither."

She whirled to face him, her cheeks flushed. "Kurun! You followed me. How dare you!" Her fingers closed around the Talisman, thrust it forward like a ward.

But the crude-proportioned alder dragon had no effect on the kind of magic this dark-eyed fisherman worked. It was too subtle, too tender a sort of conjuring. Such an arcane yet common mystery required only time and contact to come to full flower.

And it was very nearly the only form of sorcery that even the Sisterhood had never considered banishing.

A good thing, too—for it was a force older and far stronger, more elemental than any mere religion.

Still, the young Sister and the slightly-younger fisher had struggled against it. They'd fought and denied it. They'd never given in, yet never come to terms with it, either.

Now, Yorub turned her back to him—remembering, craving his touch. She recalled the softness of his lips, that one time they had met her own.

She remembered and she found herself very nearly hating—Kurun and herself.

"You followed," she repeated, not seeing his head move in denial.

Aware of her near-nakedness, Yorub wrapped her arms around herself and closed her eyes. The ache inside her grew; her training allowed no room to doubt its source.

The Link was strong and growing, the Call genuine.

"No," Kurun said at last, distracting her. Pebbles crunched, complaining beneath his boots as he stepped up to her side. "I could not sleep. Felt drawn here—summoned, Yori."

"Don't call me that! You have no right!"

"I know." Kurun swallowed, his eyes fell then rose slowly with remorse. "But tonight—it's like what I've heard you describe. Like the Sisterhood experience; like the Call!"

"Ridiculous." She snorted.

"I had to come here. There was no resisting it. I had to be here. Just as you did, it seems."

"You really think a Seadrake would Call the likes of you?"

Kurun shrugged. His gaze met hers, his thin lips parted slightly. Then a nervous gesture came, one she had seen a few times. His strong right hand wet its fingertips on his lips then brushed non-existent stray hairs from his forehead.

Despite herself, she smiled.

"I felt it," Kurun insisted. "Deep in my soul. On my honour, it's not mere restlessness or—anything else. I felt—I feel it, Yori. Now and growing stronger—out there in the water. What else could it be?"

She pursed her lips, afraid of the answer.

"Not possible," she maintained through clenched teeth. "No training, no Oath or Talisman to facilitate—and you're a man! How—and why would a Seadrake make Link with you?"

He saw something.

Following his gaze, she saw it too.

"Go," she told him, pushing against his chest. "Leave now, Kurun. Or the Drake will be displeased. Only a Sister may commune—"

"As only Sisters are Called?" The fisher stood his ground. "It—he—wants us both to approach. You feel it; don't lie to me, to him—or to yourself, Yori."

"He'll be outraged!"

A frightful, garish image flashed through Yorub's mind: Kurun crushed beneath the clawed forelimbs of the Purple One, blood pouring from his mouth and nose, something pink and slimy oozing into the wet sand from gaping puncture wounds about his head.

But this, she knew with dismay, was only the product of her own fear and swirling, guilty imaginings.

The True Vision, the hallmark of an Active Link slipped around her like a solemn and gentle cloak. It was so detailed, so intense and yet so kind that she automatically accepted its source.

"He's come here to die." Her voice was distant, a stunned murmur. "We must go to him. Do what we can to ease him. Hurry, Kurun!"

They climbed down to the beach to meet the dying dragon.

Both of them staggered, eyes wide as the great creature emerged from the surf. The Purple One was a full twenty feet tall and longer than five of the Alder-folk's finest ships laid end to end. The wide golden eyes made a startling contrast to his thick, armour-plated skin.

But those moist eyes were glazed, full of pain.

His bellow was massive, but more sad than menacing.

The young pair quivered with an understanding more terrible than fear.

Yorub touched her chest, aware that her formal tunic was back in her cottage. Her simple nightshirt seemed so inadequate a costume for her first lone meeting with a Sacred One.

Yet she was not alone.

She turned her head.

Kurun looked back at her, as full of shame and remorse—and as ready to shoulder blame—as she.


Yorub trudged back along the coastline, rounded the bend in the cove that shielded the dragon's resting spot from the village. She squinted at the sunlight dancing along the bright clean waters. It was here that Kurun's father and the others had reached shore, two long and dangerous hours after their new boat had inexplicably capsized.

The Sister gritted her teeth, shifted the pack on her back and hurried along.

Kurun still sat on a flattened slab of stone, one leg

dangling as if unconcerned. But as she approached, she saw the fisher's rigid backbone and tightly drawn face.

A short way off, the Seadrake lay sprawled upon the uneven sand and rock. His horned face rested heavily on his forelimbs, his heavy tail motionless except for the fitful buffeting of the incoming surf. The ugly, reddish lesions were spreading rapidly and Yorub knew, as she had all along, that the medicine she'd brought would do no good.

The two of them had been unable to keep all of the suffering Purple One's flesh moist and she had first planned to bring the villagers, to enlist every able set of hands and every bucket in protecting the great creature from the sun.

But the Sacred One had refused.

In no uncertain terms, the full force of the Link had made it clear that only she and Kurun were permitted here. In fact, they were required—ordered, gently but firmly, to witness this terrible sight.

The reason was as obvious as the punishment was subtle. As such, it was exactly the sort of thing one might expect from the Sacred Ones. The connection between the Sisterhood and the Purple Dragons went beyond magical communication. They were more than allies; more than two groups in a permanent, unbreakable union.

Yorub tugged the bottom of her tunic and adjusted her sword buckle as she walked. She halted at the fisher's side. "He has not moved?"

He exhaled. "Not a twitch. If dragons twitch. Do they?"

"Not a time for jokes, Kurun."

"I know." The ghost of a smile played across his face. "What did you tell the Elders?"

"What I was instructed to." She put down her pack, shook her head. "No one will come this way, nor will any fishing boats go out. Your family knows you are with me, assisting in an important and very secret ritual. They imagine it a singular honour! I sent a sealed message to the Capital, as well. Perhaps the regional Sister Leader will advance her schedule and hurry here. Not that Bemba will have any more effect on things than I!"

"No hope?"

"Do you see reason for any?" She closed her eyes. "By the Goddess, I do feel overmatched! There will be massed prayer and fasting this evening throughout the village."

"But they don't know what they're praying for?" He turned his head, cocked his brow at the motionless drake.

"General prayers. Health and joy to all the Sacred Ones of the Sea."

Kurun nodded, rose to stretch himself.

285

"This is our fault," she told him suddenly. "Ours, though mostly mine. My Vows—"

Kurun took a halting step forward. He raised a hand to her cheek then paused and looked past her. His gaze met a huge gold eye and his hand withdrew. He nodded to the Seadrake and the Purple One rumbled painfully.

"We stopped ourselves," he said solemnly, staring at the dying giant.

"I didn't want to stop!" Yorub hissed. She looked at her feet and began to weep. "I wished to go on—to break all Oaths!"

"But you did not." The fisher grimaced, drawn slowly toward the beast's great claws. "You held onto your faith, your duty. Even in the face of temptation, Yori. That has to mean something!"

"My duties." She tossed her shaved head, spat in the sand. "I neglected them. The next day, your father and the others—the new boat—I should've been there—to bless the craft in the proper manner, affix a Talisman to its bow. The accident would never have happened!"

"You don't know that." Kurun moved closer to the dragon.

"Well, at the least, the Drakes would've been there when the danger came."

Kurun shook his head, took another step toward razor-sharp, broadsword-sized claws. "They knew the risk of taking out an unblessed boat. They were simply impatient. And nobody died, Goddess be Praised!"

"I wasn't even ill!" she howled, only now seeing how close the young man had come to their dying dragon.

"You were heartsick," Kurun answered.

"I was weak and foolish. I sat in my bed all that day—wishing, wanting to die. To die, Kurun! When my village, my people were at risk!"

They both stared, watched the dragon raise its head. A forelimb moved.

"See?" Kurun babbled, halfway between humour and hysteria. "They do twitch!"

The armoured back of the forelimb flicked, struck him solidly in the shoulder and sent the fisher flying. He landed with a thud and looked up, frozen with fear.

"Kurun!" Yorub sprinted to his side, fumbling for her sword as she went. "No! It's me you want! He's innocent. I put those fisher-folk in peril. No!"

The Sacred One masked his thoughts now, though his posture made things seem clear enough. A pair of spear-like claws lingered no more than a hand's width above Kurun's face.

It was Yorub's worst fantasy come true, if only in its opening stages.

She ducked beneath the sickly creature's lumbering claws and astonished herself by shouldering the massive forelimb aside. Too fast to think it through, she grabbed the fisher by the shoulders and dragged him to the base of the nearest rock outcropping. Too desperate to be gentle, she flung him down and spun, drawing her sword in the same motion.

It was of course a Blessed Weapon, able (so it was said) to penetrate dragon armour—though certainly never intended for use one of the Purple Kind.

The huge Seadrake loomed over her, blotting out the still-rising sun. He screamed and roared like a thing gone mad, displayed a large assortment of long sharp teeth and a twisting, forked tongue.

"Yes!" She suddenly exclaimed. "I love him! More so than is seemly for a Dragon Sister, perhaps. But I throw off my shame—here, now! I reject it, do you hear? I *reject* it! Even in your presence, Sacred One! *Especially* in your presence."

Yorub paused, astonished at herself. She glanced back, saw Kurun sitting up to listen, no fear on his face. She waited, gave the Seadrake every chance to strike.

"I would die for him—or with him, if I must. But I will *not* feel shame for loving him!"

She lowered her weapon, slipped it carefully into its sheath. Her voice was strong and steady, surprising even herself.

"I also love the Sisterhood and the Way. And our Link, Sacred One. I will not harm you—not to save myself, or even him. Not even if you are mad with pain. Instead, I offer you my open heart—and two lives, still-young and promising. In return, I make but one request: Stop this foolish sulking. Stop it, Sacred One—and *live!*"

"And so," the elderly figure huffed," your 'dying' dragon had a swift and remarkable recovery?"

Yorub blinked at the Sister Leader's absolute lack of surprise. She watched Bemba hobble another couple feet along the coastline.

The old woman smiled, gestured. "You think you are the only Sister ever tested? Oh, child! We can't afford to renounce the instinct to love—even if it was within our power, which it is not. And we don't. We embrace it, as a vital part of ourselves. Only we do so in ways few ordinary people readily grasp—that is all. How else can we hope to govern well, for example? How else, if not through love?

Only certain ways of *expressing* it—sex and so forth—do we put aside. But for us—and all that feels—love is the great wonder and necessity of the ages!"

Yorub nodded, experiencing for an instant a shadow of the warm understanding the Purple One had given her as a parting gift—had given them both, in fact, as she and Kurun stood on that very spot, watching the Seadrake's wounds close and the lesions heal themselves.

"Where is this fisher today?" Bemba of Ilfer's Ridge asked after a quiet moment. "This man whom a Seadrake Called?"

"Out there with his father and others, in their new boat—it's one I have fully Blessed." Yorub brought her arm around, a sweeping gesture that carried the Sister Leader's gaze far out to sea with it.

Several boats bobbed on the horizon, heading out. Among them, two or three Seadrakes sported protectively. The distance was already too great to let mortal eyes discern which (if any) of the Purple Ones had been beached here, the week before.

"They shall return at nightfall," she continued. Then, slowly she asked, "Honoured Sister? If it is not too bold— were you ever so tested? I mean—have you ever—that is, did anyone—?"

A distant, unfocused look came over the old woman's wrinkled face. A faint smile appeared as she stood with Yorub and gazed out at the flotilla of boats and dragons.

Regardless of the exact wording of Yorub of Oyon's question, it was answer enough.